THE OAR OF
ODYSSEUS

Richard M. Bank

THE OAR OF ODYSSEUS

Addison & Highsmith

Addison & Highsmith Publishers

Las Vegas ◊ Chicago ◊ Palm Beach

Published in the United States of America by
Histria Books, a division of Histria LLC
7181 N. Hualapai Way, Ste. 130-86
Las Vegas, NV 89166 USA
HistriaBooks.com

Addison & Highsmith is an imprint of Histria Books. Titles published under the imprints of Histria Books are distributed worldwide.

Library of Congress Control Number: 2021931048

ISBN 978-1-59211-088-9 (hardcover)
ISBN 978-1-59211-153-4 (softbound)
ISBN 978-1-59211-226-5 (eBook)

TO LAURA

THE LOVE OF MY LIFE

ARCHAIC TORSO OF APOLLO

We cannot fathom his mysterious head,
Through the veiled eyes no flickering ray is sent:
But from his torso gleaming light is shed
As from a candelabrum; inward bent

His glance there glows and lingers. Otherwise
The round breast would not blind you with its grace,
Nor could the soft-curved circle of the thighs
Steal to the arc whence issues a new race.

Nor could this stark and stunted stone display
Vibrance beneath the shoulders heavy bar,
Nor shine like fur upon a beast of prey,
Nor break forth from its lines like a great star —

There is no spot that does not bind you fast
And transport you back, back to a far past.

— Rainer Maria Rilke (translated by Jessie Lemont)
after encountering an unfinished sculpture of Apollo

"Art in progress is like life, underway but still full of possibilities."

— Penelope Bauer

CHAPTER 1

H er acceptance letter arrived on Friday, May 5, and Penelope was ready to party. She would not be alone. Not even dark yet, and she had already heard a few celebratory gunshots. *Cinco de Mayo* was a big deal in northern New Mexico or at least a good excuse to drink. Apparently, on that day in 1862, the Mexicans won a battle that all but expelled the French from their country. What were the French doing in Mexico anyway, she often wondered. But not tonight. Tonight all she cared about was the quality, and the quantity, of the margaritas.

But as she sat on the barstool at Harry's, nursing her second silver coin, her mood turned bittersweet. She would graduate in a week, marking the end of her college career at the small liberal arts school in Santa Fe — a school that too would be marking its end. Plagued by financial mismanagement, or worse, the College of St. Frances had sold out, literally, to a somewhat shady private educational outfit that planned to open a for-profit law school. Actually, she would be attending one of two graduation ceremonies, hers being the "alternative" organized by a group of students. An impotent protest at this point, but a final middle finger salute to the slimy College President and his lackeys, who would be hosting the sure to be sparsely attended "official" ceremony.

Her mood brightened a bit when she remembered that her mentor, Dr. A. Michael Ambros, was to deliver the commencement address. Having seen the writing on the wall, Michael — as he insisted his students call him — tendered his resignation the previous year in a letter highly critical of the College's Administration and Board. Penelope missed him. He was the reason she had decided to pursue a doctorate in classics, and no doubt largely responsible for the acceptance letter from the program at Boston University. That letter now rested safely on her desk under the bronze statuette of the goddess Artemis, his gift to her when he left the College. She had not seen or talked to him since he had encouraged her to apply to BU, promising to lobby his contacts there and write her a glowing letter of recommendation. She had to give him something special before she left for Boston. But what?

"Another?"

Penny looked up into the bartender's warm smile and giggled. "God, no. I'd never make it home. Hey, any ideas about what I could give my favorite professor, you know, as a thank-you gift?"

"The guy who's speaking at your graduation?"

"Wow! How did you know that? You should be the one going to grad school, Sheryl."

"Not me, bright eyes," Sheryl said as she reached down for a copy of the local paper, dropping it on the bar. "There was a story about him in the *Reporter*."

Sure enough. Penny was staring down at Michael's picture as Sheryl continued. "And it's not like you've never talked about him. Listening to you, one would think the man walked on water. I'm sure you'll think of something to offer that guy if you haven't already." Smirking, she slowly ran a finger around his face on the page.

"Whatever do you mean?" Penny replied, failing to suppress another giggle.

It was Sheryl's turn to laugh. "You know *exactly* what I mean. Sure you don't want another?"

"Maybe one more."

ΩΩΩ

Penelope looked at the clock — again. Less than 10 minutes had passed since the last time, although it felt more like half an hour. Her parents wouldn't pick her up for another 45 minutes. Restlessly pacing about her little casita, she found herself staring into the full-length mirror on the bathroom door and sighing in utter frustration. Why put the mirror on the inside of the door? Who would get dressed in that tiny bathroom? To use the mirror, she had to open the door wide, giving visitors an unflattering, if honest, impression of her housekeeping skills. Still, she could not have asked for a better living situation. It had been good to get away from campus for her final year. She valued the privacy it afforded, giving her the time and space for some serious introspection. Not to mention that it was walking distance to Harry's, she giggled. The couple she rented from had been kind and generous too; they could have charged twice what she paid.

She fluffed her shoulder-length waves of reddish hair — what others called strawberry blonde, much to her displeasure. Thank God she didn't have to wear a mortarboard. In fact, there would be few students in graduation garb of any sort at her ceremony, given the College Administration's mercenary scheme on behalf of the new owners. To attend the "official" graduation, students were required to purchase robes and caps from the College bookstore at highly inflated prices. Of course, the attempt to extract every last nickel from already disgruntled students backfired, fueling efforts to organize the alternative ceremony.

Her father was suspicious of alternatives. A very conventional and practical man, shaped perhaps by his Germanic roots, he questioned much of Penelope's academic career and aspirations. She was Daddy's little girl, and he worried about her life in liberal Santa Fe, and God forbid, Boston! And the classics? She might as well become a poet or a musician. Little did he know that, if she'd had the talent, she would have relished either of those paths. Her mother, on the other hand, was a fiery Irish lass, with wild dreams and flaming red hair, full of spirit and determination — what her father called "stubbornness." They were an odd pair, but deeply in love with each other and their only child.

She was glad they were here, Frank and Siobhan Bauer. Penny met them last evening at the cute B&B near downtown she had found for them, and they walked from there to Pranzo's for dinner. Siobhan insisted that they order a bottle of wine, ignoring her husband's stern look. Frank could not believe his daughter had just turned 22, let alone 21. He was quiet the whole evening, his brooding gray-blue eyes giving nothing away but his mood. Tired from the drive from Ruidoso, surely, but also concerned. Penny knew her father could worry about anything, but tonight it was probably the realization that she was leaving New Mexico, really leaving, and soon. She circled her fork in her fettuccine and grinned, knowing she could assuage his mood, at least temporarily, with a long father-daughter hug when she said goodnight.

Her mother, on the other hand, could not have been more excited. "Boston is such a unique city! Classics — such an interesting field of study! And your Aunt Alice is so happy that you'll be staying with her! Just don't mention the Irish sheep rustlers. As you know, my sister and I hold very different views of that history." Penny knew. Her mother the anarchist was proud to be descended from such noble souls. In her mind, they were liberators of sheep, for the men claiming ownership were English lords. Throughout it all, Penny marveled at the way her mother's azure eyes sparkled — as if her daughter had been blessed with the enchanted journey that might have once been Siobhan's own dream.

Still at the mirror, staring at her no-nonsense face, tightly framed by her tumbling locks, she saw bits of both her parents: her lower lip full like her mother's, not so lucky with her upper lip or her nose, one a little slender, the other a little wide, both inherited from her father. And she'd never be a model with her sturdy cheekbones. Just then a cloud blocked the sun and her eyes changed color, from emerald green to a much paler jade, flecked as always with gold or yellow or brown, depending on the light. Her latest boyfriend said her eyes were the color of wet rocks. She smiled. Maybe he would become a poet. All in all, she liked her looks and her athletic body; they suited her. A glimpse of the statue of Artemis reflected at the mirror's edge made her think of Amazons, and her smile broadened. *I'm petite for an Amazon,* she thought as she heard the knock at the door, *but an Amazon just the same!*

ΩΩΩ

Penelope was sitting with her fellow graduates in the orchestra section of the Santa Fe Opera, now covered against the rain and sun but still open to the air. She was fidgeting a little, struggling to pull down the hem of her sky-blue belted sundress. Standing it fell mid-thigh; sitting was another matter. But it was her favorite summer dress, and it was such a lovely warm and sunny day.

She was only half-listening to Santa Fe's Mayor, offering greetings and such to the assembled multitude, including a sizable contingent of journalists. The Opera had long been the venue for CSF's graduations, he said, but pleading poverty, President Steward had canceled this year's reservation. The impending sale of the College to the Kinslaw Group was announced shortly thereafter, and then it was discovered that Steward had accepted a senior executive position at Kinslaw. The whole deal smelled of corruption and betrayal, especially as the City of Santa Fe's prior bid to acquire CSF had been rejected. For many in the community, President Steward became "President Sewer," and support grew quickly, both on and off campus, for the alternative graduation ceremony proposed by a group of graduating seniors. Happily, two of those seniors had parents on the Opera's Board of Directors, and said the Mayor, "Well, here we are."

Penny already knew this story. Her thoughts were elsewhere, replaying her family's earlier encounter with Michael. She'd been immensely proud to introduce her parents to him in their matching linen suits and calfskin western boots, set off by just a touch of turquoise: her father's bolo tie, her mother's delicate squash blossom necklace. While their lives in Ruidoso were far removed from that of a classics scholar, the conversation was relaxed and congenial. Even when her father asked the inevitable question about her future prospects, his tone, far from confrontational, expressed genuine curiosity. And Michael's response was as intriguing as it was surprising and embarrassing.

"I hope my little talk today will provide you an answer," he said, the twinkle in his dark eyes, really the only distinct part of his face, the rest shielded by a full gray beard and his shaggy mop of silver hair. Dressed in an ancient corduroy suit over a beige shirt open at the collar, with gray hairs sprouting from there as well, he looked every bit the retired academic. "But I will say this. Your daughter has an intellect worthy of Plato's Academy, although as a woman, she would never have been admitted." The way he said "woman" as his eyes found hers had sent chills down her spine.

"But she has something far more valuable," he continued. "Courage. The courage to open herself to life, to embrace its joys and its sorrows, to risk loving and being loved. The courage of self-reflection, to know herself, and to choose always her better self. And, perhaps most important, the courage to create." Then, looking first to Frank and then Siobhan, "Your love and care has given her this; you both should be very proud. And you can trust that your daughter will leave an indelible mark in this world." With that, he shook her father's hand, kissed her mother's cheek, smiled at Penny, as she stood there stunned and blushing the color of her mother's hair, and bid them all farewell.

Just then she heard his name. The Mayor was introducing him, and Penny found herself applauding, and cheering, and as one body, rising with her fellow graduates as Michael walked to the lectern, where he shook the Mayor's hand, and if she wasn't mistaken, blushed — something she had never seen before. Revenge was sweet, indeed, she thought playfully. And then he spoke, accompanied by pin- dropping silence, the occasional cough, the predictable chuckle, and the soft sweet notes of the house finches high up in the metalwork above the stage.

"Please... please be seated. I'm a bit overwhelmed by this reception, and thoroughly humbled. And as my students know, humility is not my strong suit. Needless to say, I am deeply honored by the opportunity afforded me to speak with all of you today. As is the usual practice of a commencement speaker, I will begin by acknowledging the members of the College's Board and the representatives of its Administration; only at this ceremony, I happily acknowledge them by their absence. For they have proved themselves unworthy of sharing this day with us.

"On the other hand, we should be profoundly grateful for the generosity and goodwill of the larger community of Santa Fe in helping to give these students and their beloved College a proper send-off. That, of course, is why we are here. First and foremost, to celebrate the accomplishments of the graduates seated before us, and equally to honor the support and sacrifices of their families and friends. But we are also gathered together for another kind of celebration — a wake, if you will, and I cannot overstate the importance of remembering the College of St. Frances, its purpose, and its mission. Let me tell you why.

"Institutions like the College of St. Frances are disappearing across the land as corporations like the Kinslaw Group step in to fill the breach — all part of a larger trend that might be called the commodification of higher education. A college degree has become a product, marketed as a means to what many have come to regard as the good life, that is, one or another variant of the American Dream.

"Consider Kinslaw's plans for its law school. Students will likely be lured with promises of exciting careers, six-figure salaries, and country club memberships. But, in fact, its graduates have a dismal track record of passing the bar exam, let alone realizing their material vision of the good life. I have no evidence to indict the curriculum or the instructors; they may, in fact, be teaching the skills necessary to the practice of law. I will suggest, however, that most of Kinslaw's recruits are unqualified or unsuited to study law, because the only standard for admission is the ability to pay the tuition and fees. And almost all of its recruits will secure these funds through federal student loans, money Kinslaw will pocket as soon as it is distributed. After three years, these students will graduate with a law degree, but with little chance of ever practicing law, and shouldered with crushing debt that likely will never be repaid. Kinslaw's business plan, in short, is this: sell the students a worthless degree, ruin them financially, and bilk literally millions of dollars from U.S. taxpayers. Sadly, this is perfectly legal and the general *modus operandi* of all for-profit colleges. Simply put, for-profit educational institutions are, as advertised, for profit, that is, not for students.

"Liberal arts colleges like the College of St. Frances follow a different model. Ideally, their mission is all about students, their purpose to improve the lives of those who enter their doors. Earlier today, I was approached by the father of one of our graduates...."

Michael's eyes found Penny's just as she swallowed a gasp and blushed an even darker shade of red. "He wanted to know what a degree in the humanities would do for his daughter's prospects and how she could earn a living. I could have told him about the growing body of research that finds a liberal arts education well-suited for adapting to our rapidly changing social and economic conditions. But coming from me, that would have been disingenuous. Because I believe that a liberal arts education is useless when judged against a material standard of the good life. Students are drawn to the liberal arts by a different vision of the good life, a vision rooted in an understanding of what it means to be human, or more precisely, humane. Their studies help them to discover that human beings need not be swayed by advertisers and marketers, who seek to ensnare them in the consumption-driven trap of the American Dream. They experience, many for the first time, the pleasures of leading a genuinely good life, a moral life, and are thereby empowered, liberated from the need to acquire the newest iPhone, free to make their own life choices, to dance to their own drummer. To all the parents of today's graduates I can say this: whatever paths your daughters and sons choose, they will choose with care and compassion. There will be detours and missteps, surely, but by their presence here today, at this alternative ceremony — which they envisioned, demanded, and forged — they have demonstrated the strength of character that will see them through their lives, lives that have been and will continue to be ennobled by having studied the liberating arts.

"Of course, colleges like CSF are not immune to the forces of commodification. Such schools are increasingly diverted from their mission by ever greater numbers of high salaried administrators, who compete for students with new recreation centers and other amenities. And the price of tuition, already exorbitant, continues to rise. These trends will persist so long as the forces of commodification are ascendant. But we must not give up hope.

"As I stand before you, I am an old man and a classics scholar. In many ways, I have lived among the ancient Greeks, who taught that as we approach death, the powers of prophecy are heightened. Hear, then, my vision of the future. Artemis, my favorite god in the pantheon of Olympus, is often depicted as a huntress, bow and arrow in hand, standing over a felled deer. I have always believed she was hunting bigger game, ever seeking truth and justice. And now, in our time of peril, she is raising an army of strong young women — an army of Amazons, if you will, devoted to the defense of the values of Olympus, the values of the good life, the values engendered by the liberal arts. We see this all around us, do we not? Young women raising their voices, demanding to be heard in the service of truth and justice. Let this be a warning to those who find themselves mired in the Sewer across town: Kinslaw will be the target of the first arrow to fly in the epic struggle ahead. May the memory of CSF live long in the hearts and minds of these chosen few before us, the last graduates of the College of St. Frances!"

In the moment of stunned silence before she joined the riotous standing ovation, Penelope knew the farewell gift Michael deserved and she would bestow.

ΩΩΩ

Penny was pacing the confines of the small casita that was to be her home for one last night. She was leaving for Boston the following evening, having already shipped all of her books and belongings, save what she could carry on the plane. She'd eaten or tossed the contents of her refrigerator, which now just housed an $80 bottle of champagne and two cheap wine glasses. She'd had to use the credit card her father gave her for emergencies to buy the wine — she thought of it as an emergency of sorts. Her father, she knew, was unlikely to see it that way.

She looked again at the spot on her empty bookshelf, where her clock had once rested, then at her watch, the hands of which had frozen at 6:15. She had no idea what time it was, time seemingly choosing this evening to desert her. Looking out her front door, she watched the last sliver of sun dip behind the Jemez Mountains. That would make it 8 p.m., wouldn't it? Maybe Michael never got her email. She would have preferred to text him, but he didn't own a cell phone. All her plans, all this anxiety for nothing!

She tried to recall exactly what she'd written. *Please come to my place, 8 p.m. on Sunday to share a bottle of champagne. I've attached a map. No need to reply unless you can't make it.* Something like that. Why didn't she ask him to reply, in any event? Dumb. But then she saw a pair of headlights turning up the distant drive. She was at once relieved and even more anxious. And in her overwrought state, she imagined the two lights tightly focused in a single beam, aimed directly at her. Must be some new kind of bulb.

As Michael pulled up in front, she took a series of deep breaths, waiting for him on the porch at her open door, not wanting to risk a stumble on the steps. Dressed in what he always wore when teaching, a faded canvas shirt and jeans, he made his way up the stairs, his eyes never leaving hers. For an instant she felt those eyes, tightly focused, as an echo of the headlights. But that feeling quickly faded as he reached her, bending slightly to kiss her on the cheek.

"Good evening, Penelope," he said, with a merry smile.

Penny was taken aback, first by the kiss, then by his amusement at her expense. "Are you laughing at me?"

"I'm trying very hard not to. Should I not have kissed your cheek?"

Flustered, she struggled to recover some semblance of composure. "Um... yes... no... I mean, it was fine... I was just a little shocked, that's all."

"Why, Penny? Were you shocked when I kissed your mother's cheek at graduation?"

"No, not really. But she's my mother."

"And you're her daughter and looking very lovely tonight. I liked that dress on you at graduation, and it becomes you even more in the twilight, especially when you blush. Are you going to invite me in?"

Speechless, blushing, Penny did all she could do, which was a sweeping gesture with her hand, beckoning him to enter, and closing the door after them. She watched Michael inspecting the all but deserted space, finally spotting and gently stroking the statute of Artemis standing guard on the small dining table. He turned to face her, raising his bushy eyebrows questioningly.

"To bear witness," she said, having gathered what was left of her wits. "And to accompany me on the plane tomorrow night." And then boldly, "What's going on, Michael?"

He smiled at her, a smile that could only be described as tender. "I apologize. You looked... so anxious, standing on the porch. This may sound odd, but I sensed that you would never relax until you got all that out of your system."

"So you thought you'd freak me out," she fired back at him, actually starting to relax. Perhaps he had been right.

"Something like that. Again, I'm sorry. I meant what I said, however. You look stunning this evening, all grown up, ready to take on the world."

"Thank you." She blushed again, but graciously accepted the compliment, feeling the last of her tension dissolving. She retrieved the bottle of champagne, handing it to him. "Shall we open this?" she asked, smiling and watching his reaction.

His face lit up. "Wow, Reinart!" He did not disappoint her.

"Something you said in class one day. You told us Reinart was the best champagne you'd ever tasted, that you'd only had it once while traveling through France in 1897." She giggled. "It was the first time you cracked wise about your age, so it stuck in my memory."

"A slip of the tongue, that," Michael mumbled to himself, popping the cork.

"What?" she asked, having not quite heard him, as she placed the chilled wine glasses on the table.

A dismissive shake of his head, then looking to her with a bright smile. "Shall I pour?"

"Of course! I thought we might alternate toasts. I'll go first." Carefully lifting her glass, in a bold ringing voice, "To friendship... deep and lasting!"

They clinked and sipped. "Oh my...." Michael moaned. "Better even than I remember." Lowering his gaze to meet hers, she, of course, blushed. "Very extravagant. Thank you."

"Some things require extravagance," she replied, offering him a shy smile. "Ok, your turn."

"Hmmm. To your journey to Ithaca." He raised his glass to her puzzled look.

"But I'm going to Boston, not Ithaca."

"Look it up, a modern Greek poet, Cavafy. Believe me, if anyone is going to Ithaca, it's you."

She shrugged her shoulders, touched her glass to his, and drained it. "I need a full glass for my next toast," she said, a measure of anxiety returning, which did not go unnoticed by Michael as he slowly filled both glasses again. Penny took a deep breath, held her glass aloft, and proposed the toast she'd been thinking about since graduation. "To an unbridled night of passion."

It was Michael's turn to be taken aback. He stared at her raised glass, the sparkling bubbles resisting the fading light, then at her face, steady and resolute, thwarting his attempt to read her. She did not blush; in fact, it was the palest he'd ever seen her. He set his glass on the table, taking one of the two facing chairs. "Can we talk about this?"

She hesitated a beat, quietly sighed, but took the other chair, the statue of Artemis between them, looking on. "Ok, but I'll talk first." Michael's reaction was not exactly what she'd hoped, but neither was it unexpected, and Penny had spent a long time thinking hard about what she would say. Even so, she took her time now; she wanted to get it right. Finally, she began, facing him squarely, unashamed, confident in her decision. "I'll admit that until very recently I had not considered anything like this. You are, after all, old enough to be my grandfather." She smirked at him.

He smiled back at her. "You'd be amazed at how old I am."

"How old are you?" she asked, genuinely curious.

"Now that would be telling." His turn to smirk.

"Whatever," she sighed, regaining her focus with a deep breath. "I've never known anyone like you. So caring and giving of yourself. You've been my teacher and my mentor; you've enriched my life in so many ways. Throughout it all you have been nothing but proper and professional toward me, but a girl knows when she's desired." She raised her hand, checking his attempt to speak. "But I am not your student any more. I have been accepted to graduate school. As you said, all grown up. We are on an equal footing now, no power dynamics to trouble us." Smiling to herself and shaking her head. "You probably understood all this before I did. I saw how you looked at me at graduation."

Michael chuckled. "Well, it's spring. You know, birds nesting, bees buzzing, sap rising," lifting an eyebrow provocatively.

"Ok, then. Here's how I see the situation. You want me and probably have for some time. And I want desperately to give you something special in return for everything you've given me. We are friends now, nothing more, and tonight I want, I truly want, to be your friend... with benefits." Giving him a shy smile, she lifted her glass again, holding it high and steady.

"You really don't know what you might be getting into here... there could be consequences..."

She cut him off. "I am a 22-year-old woman in 2018 America; I take precautions for God's sake! And, if I may use a tortured metaphor, a skill I learned from you, by the way, I might be a spring chicken, but your rooster feathers have faded considerably." Smirking once more. "You have given me so much, please let me give you this... please."

Michael could see that she was sincere and determined, her glass still raised. Resigned, he lifted his own, gently touching hers, and then spoke, his tone prophetic and a bit unnerving: "I will not deny you your destiny, but Fate can be a harsh and demanding mistress. You honor me beyond measure by taking such a risk."

They drank. She swallowed hard and shivered, his words testing her resolve. But then she stood and approached him. He was sitting with his long legs to the side of the table. She gently pressed herself between them, which he opened to receive her. Gazing into his eyes, she imagined a passing cloud of sadness, but definitely saw a deep and dark desire — a desire that was something more than lust. She leaned in and kissed him tenderly on the lips. Again, this time his mouth opening to her, their tongues entwining in a seductive dance. He pulled her down onto his lap, and their worlds were forever changed.

ΩΩΩ

Penny awoke alone in her bed, a bit dazed and disoriented. The room, just large enough for her double bed, was bathed in bright sunshine. Its window faced east, the drapes open; she didn't bother to close them, except in winter. Aside from the main house to the southwest, the nearest neighbors were half a mile distant. Blinking sleep away, she took a deep breath, inhaling the scent of sex, lots of sex, a smile threatening to break out interrupted by a rush of adrenaline. Where's Michael? She kicked away the sheet, stumbled out of bed, calling out his name — more like a croak, her mouth dry, her voice tight. Three quick steps through the open bedroom door, immediately catching the glint of sun off metal through the picture window, and she relaxed. Michael's car — he was still near.

She walked about, calmer now, stretching her naked limbs, an odd combination of limber and sore, as if cooling down after a bike ride up the mountain. She spied her dress, carefully draped over the straight-backed chair, her blue lace panties folded neatly atop. Michael must have cleaned up in here, she thought, giggling as the image of him tearing off her clothes passed before her eyes. He's probably taking a walk, she thought. Just as well, because she really needed a shower.

Scrubbed clean, refreshed, the soothing warm water washing over her, Penny was lost in thought, trying to process the events of the previous night. She needed to understand things. More than once she'd been told she lived too much in her head, usually from soon-to-be ex-boyfriends. She was a whiz at math, at anything analytical, really. But those skills weren't helping her now. Not that she and Michael had done anything she hadn't done before, but everything about the experience was different. The best she could do was to liken it to a symphony. Four movements, differing in style and pace, each with its own climax — a fucking symphony, she thought, giggling.

But no. They hadn't fucked at all — she knew what that felt like. Pleasant, exciting even, but she had always felt a degree of detachment. This time, the observant part of her had been lost, silenced. She had been completely swept up, as if caught in the current of a raging river. Gasping, she recalled the image of the Nile, laying down its fertile delta, when he entered her for the first time. And just then, that single instant of blinding white light, more a feeling than a flash — but in any event, not like the soft light enveloping them throughout, swirling around them as if blown about by a gentle breeze.

The light — my God, what was that about? There should not have been any light. Her flight to Boston fell on the new moon — she'd noted that when she bought her ticket. Whatever tiny crescent of moon remaining would have been visible, if at all, just before dawn. No lights were on in the casita, no light reached them from the city, and no moon. It should have been pitch black. Strange.

"Hello! I've got breakfast."

The sound of Michael's voice evoked a veritable range of feelings, but anxiety the most prominent. This would be a morning after like no other. Distracted from her musings and quickly drying herself with the remaining fresh towel — one of two she had strategically left unpacked — she wondered how she would get to her clothes laid out in the bedroom. Peeking around the bathroom door, she saw Michael fussing at the kitchen counter and scurried to the bedroom, her head down. If she couldn't see him, he couldn't see her — an artifact of magical thinking that anxious moments often produced.

"It's not like I haven't seen you naked," he called after her, laughing.

Oddly, the fact that he had seen her pleased her for reasons she had no time to explore. She pulled on her jeans and a soft cotton CSF hoody over clean bra and panties, her feet bare for the moment, and her hair hanging wet. Gathering herself, taking a deep breath, she left the relative safety of her bedroom to face she knew not what.

She was greeted by Michael's smile, but there was sadness in his eyes. "I walked over to Harry's," he said. "Hope you like breakfast burritos and coffee. It's all I could think of that wouldn't require plates or utensils."

She stood stock-still, watching him organize their meal on the table, and when he again looked up at her, she asked, "What's wrong?"

Gazing at her for a long moment, cataloging every detail of her face before he spoke. "We need to talk." He pulled out a chair for her; she remained standing.

"Sounds serious."

"It is, but it's not what you think. Can we sit?" He stood holding the chair for her until she finally accepted his invitation. Michael sat across from her, lifting the lid from his coffee, taking a sip.

That he presumed to know what she was thinking annoyed her, and she let that mask her real fear when she spoke. "Pray tell, what exactly am I thinking?"

"You think that I'm going to say that last night was a mistake... that it never should have happened."

Penny sat there, mouth open, but no words coming out. Yes, that's exactly what she thought. After a minute that felt like an hour, she responded. "So, you read minds as well as books."

"I just know you, Penny."

It's true, she thought, recalling the way he knew to calm her the night before. Feeling like she should lighten the mood, she shrugged her shoulders playfully and smiled. "Are you telling me all the mystery is gone after one night?"

He returned her smile and chuckled. "On the contrary, the mysteries are just beginning," he said, breathing deeply to gather himself. "Something wonderful happened last night, Penelope. For both of us, I think, but certainly for me. Something I cannot find the words to articulate fully."

Oh! Just like me, she thought.

"You have given me the greatest gift a man can receive from a woman, a gift worthy of a god. But our relationship, if that's what we call it, will likely anger some very powerful individuals, with whom I have long-standing ties. I cannot tell you the whole story now because to do so could place you in grave danger. And if anything were to happen to you, I would never forgive myself."

Penny sat stunned, three times over. Greatest gift... powerful individuals... grave danger? What the fuck? Of all the things he might have told her, she could have never expected this.

"Let me try to explain the situation with an analogy," he all but pleaded. "Imagine that I'm a playwright, and just as the play is set to open, or even after it has, I unilaterally decide to change the script. The producer, the director, the actors might all be angry, even if the change is a good one. My task is to convince them that the change is in fact good, and that there were legitimate reasons for not discussing it with them beforehand. This will take me some time, a month or two. After that, I promise to come to Boston and tell you everything. You need to trust me here, Penny. Can you do that? Can you trust me?"

All kinds of wild scenarios were running through Penny's mind. Who are these people? The Russian Mafia? The CIA? Why can't we go to the police? And who is this man I just slept with? Can I trust him?

That question stopped her. She had to banish all the crazy possibilities from her mind and focus on what she knew. To his credit,

Michael waited patiently as she deliberated. He did know her, that she couldn't just answer blindly, that she had to think it through.

Here was a man, devoted to his students, to their liberation from false gods — false in the sense that they represented beliefs and values fed to them by parents and schools and screens of all kinds before they were capable of judging for themselves. He provided the space and the tools for them to test their values. Michael rarely cared what they found, so long as they were free to make and genuinely own their choices. She knew this from her own experience — and she trusted her own experience. A man so dedicated to the liberating arts could be trusted, she thought. But there was more. He cared for her, loved her even, in love with her, perhaps. She knew this too from her experience — she knew it in her gut, she knew it in her heart, and now she knew it in another part of her anatomy. She looked up at him and smiled. "Yes, I trust you," she said simply.

Michael let out the breath he had been holding and took her hands in his. "So, I do not think you are in any real peril now, but you still need to be careful. Be especially careful about who you trust." He chuckled. "Hold them at bay, at least as long as you made me wait." Turning his head toward the statue of Artemis, he continued. "Her you can trust. She's solid as a rock. Keep Artemis close and she will keep you safe. I promise."

CHAPTER 2

F inally on the plane, awaiting clearance at the Albuquerque International Sunport. Two hours to Houston, an hour layover, then four hours to Logan — with the time change, she would probably get to Aunt Alice's Cambridge Victorian sometime early tomorrow morning. She would try her best to sleep a little on the planes, but that seemed unlikely. Too much to think about. Besides, she could sleep for a week once she was settled.

Penny regretted how things had ended with Michael. The intense intimacy of the night before derailed and overshadowed by the profound and perhaps dangerous secrets now lying between them — no wonder they were shy, tentative, and even awkward with each other. At least there was one light moment when she handed him her lace panties. "You might as well keep these," she told him, "after all, I bought them for you." She smiled, remembering how much he'd blushed and how much she'd teased him about that. She was a little disappointed that he was not bold enough to sniff them in her presence, stuffing them instead in the front pocket of his jeans and promising to return them when he came to Boston. That was something to look forward to: the truth, the whole truth, and a chance to repair whatever relationship they still had. As the plane lifted from the ground and began its steep ascent, Penny set her tasks. The ride to Houston would be devoted to constructing plausible scenarios to explain what Michael told her this morning, and the longer trip to Boston reserved for the surprisingly more difficult task of discerning her own feelings for him.

She reached under the seat for her backpack and retrieved Artemis. The hard thinking ahead would require a god's help, she knew, and her own analytical skills.

Who were the "powerful individuals" with whom Michael had "long-standing ties?" Not a single individual, but a group of individuals, an organization of some kind of which he is a member, perhaps. Long-standing ties would fit with that, as would family relations, some of whom might coincidentally be powerful. What sort of organization would be angered by his relationship with a young woman? The Fraternal Order of Gay Scholars, upset that he was switching sides? The Order of Chaste Classicists, angry that he had broken his vows? She giggled. Not only was it hard to imagine Michael as either gay or chaste, but organizations of this sort would be mad at him, not her. Nothing like this would put her in "grave danger."

What could possibly place her at risk? Absently, she placed her hand on her belly, rubbing it protectively, as she tried to imagine what kind of threat she might conceivably pose. If she and Michael became seriously involved, that could threaten his heirs. Maybe he has money or valuable ancient artifacts. She looked at Artemis lying on her lap. Like you, she thought. Maybe his relatives or organizations named in his will were worried about some young gold digger cashing in at their expense. That works, she thought excitedly for a moment, but then she recalled his analogy. Apparently, these powerful individuals had reasons to presume that he would consult with them before, what? — having sex with a young woman? Why would he need anyone's permission to do that? Could he be married to a woman from some powerful family, wanting to avoid a scandal or a divorce? Would that be enough to make such people want to harm her? What could make the stakes high enough? What if she were pregnant? Looking down, she gasped, jerking her hand from her belly. *God no! That's not possible — is it?* She put her head in her hands, tears threatening, struggling to calm herself. Her reason told her not to worry. She was religious about taking her pills. Besides, Michael was older than time. A curious thought that — older than time. And there it was, in a dark part of her psyche, the image of the Nile River and its fertile plain, the blinding white light. She recalled Michael's words to her: "something wonderful happened last night... the greatest gift a man can receive from a woman...." He knew, they both knew — or at least suspected. He had tried to warn her: "there could be consequences... Fate can be a harsh and demanding mistress... you're taking such a risk." Whatever the scenario, she was not the target; it was the baby she carried. Their baby. She squeezed Artemis with both hands, lifting her close to her face, and quietly whispered. "Do whatever you must to keep us safe. Please." She hugged Artemis to her chest as the pilot announced their final approach to Houston Hobby.

She shuffled off the plane, bone-tired and dazed, making her way distractedly down the concourse toward the departure gate to Logan. A sparsely occupied bar tucked away in a small alcove elicited a grim chuckle as she thought ruefully how much she could use a drink. Not going to happen — not for a long while. Oddly, that thought cheered her. Her mind was doing what it needed to do: focusing on small practical steps, not leaping ahead to the panic-inducing reality of motherhood at 22. First things first. She would stop taking her birth control pills. Safer for the baby, probably, and if she wasn't pregnant, it would bring on her period. As if that was going to happen. Still, she needed to confirm the truth of what she had already accepted.

Too soon for a pregnancy test, surely. A couple of weeks hence, she could purchase one of those home tests, or better yet, make an appointment with a doctor. Probably not Dr. Ambros, she giggled, although he did seem to know his way around her lady parts. That brought to mind the image of Michael at the Opera praising her courage. It wasn't so much what he had said that she recalled, although she hoped she could measure up to his words — rather, the way his eyes furtively devoured her body while coolly addressing her parents. She smiled at that, slumping into a chair near the gate and closing her eyes.

Rustling sounds, sudden commotion, her eyes popped open, they were calling her plane. She must have dozed off for most of an hour. It's not like she couldn't use the rest — and she'd had such a nice dream. Lying on a white sand beach, warm Mediterranean waters lapping at her toes, watching a young girl romping in the gentle surf. Such a pretty girl, light olive complexion, long sea-soaked auburn hair, dazzling white smile. Feeling more refreshed than she deserved, Penny was actually looking forward to the flight, a four-hour opportunity to unravel her feelings for one A. Michael Ambros.

She had already dismissed the idea that Michael might be married. He was nothing if not an honorable man; he would have certainly disclosed something that significant before he joined in her farewell toast and all that followed. Even now, just thinking about what followed made her blush. That night irrecoverably altered their relationship, and not just because they were likely to have a baby together. In fact, she had to try to set that part aside in order to think clearly about her feelings. She also had to forget about his age — that was nothing more than a practical distraction from the task at hand. Of course, the task at hand, thinking clearly about her feelings, was likely an impossible undertaking, given the obvious chasm between thinking and feeling. But this was Penny's way, using her mind to understand the stirrings in her heart.

She would start with what she had discovered through experience, the distinction between fucking and what she now understood for the first time to be making love. *Poêsis*, the Greek root of poesy, or the art of poetry, also translates into English as "making." This Penny recalled from one of Michael's lectures. Making love is poetry, fucking is just fucking. She had already likened making love with Michael to music, a symphony. Again she pulled Artemis from her backpack, held her tight, communed with her. Music and poetry evoke emotions, feelings. Making love, then, is to evoke or create feelings of love. Is that what happened for her? *Eros*, another Greek word, the primordial god of love in some accounts, means longing and a kind of madness. Was Artemis grinning? If she was, it was probably because Penny had packed the sheets and Michael's towel unwashed, to preserve the scent of him, and of them together — and they now resided in the overhead bin above her. Not unlike her impulse to give Michael her panties. What was all that about if not longing and madness? She giggled. And there was that moment this morning, when she fled to her bedroom naked, pleased in the end that Michael had seen her. He saw her, truly saw her. Not like her father, who saw a little girl, or her mother, who saw her own dreams embodied in her daughter. Her thoughts of her parents in this way not unkind, but loving and sentimental. But Michael saw her naked, literally and figuratively, giving her the freedom to be who she was, to be authentic, to be complete. She seized that opportunity and reveled in it. She wanted to be authentic, for herself and for him; she felt complete with him. Why? Because she loved him. There was no other explanation. Tears were falling gently from her eyes, wetting her cheeks, as she hugged Artemis to her chest. She loved him, he loved her, and they were going to have a baby. Love they had made, truly.

ΩΩΩ

Groggy from the two hours sleep she had managed on the plane, just enough to remind her body how exhausted she was, Penny trudged toward the security exit. A stiff neck made it hard for her to read the overhead signs directing passengers to the baggage claim area and ground transportation. She only needed the latter. But as she passed through the gate and made the proper turn, she spotted a portly man dressed in a shiny well-worn polyester suit, holding a sign with "Penelope Bauer" printed in bold black letters. She approached him, more curious than anything else.

"Ms. Bauer?" he queried.

She nodded.

"Your aunt asked me to collect you." His round face jollied by a bright smile.

"Did she, now?" Curiosity gave way to apprehension, as she recalled Michael's injunction: be careful whom you trust! Spying a women's bathroom, she pointed to the entrance, offering the man a brief smile. "Let me just slip in there for a moment." Her luggage in tow, she entered and quickly called her aunt.

Alice answered on the first ring. "Penny? Are you here?"

Hearing her aunt's excited voice, she immediately relaxed. "Hi, Aunt Alice. Yes, at Logan. Did you send someone to pick me up? Looks like Santa Claus without the costume."

A hearty laugh. "That's got to be Harold. He works for a car service I use sometimes. I apologize for not warning you. Very smart of you to check."

She smiled at her aunt's praise. "Then I guess I'll see you shortly! *Adiós.*"

ΩΩΩ

Alice O'Connor was two years older than Penny's mother and regarded by both sisters as the more practical one. That said, they were very much alike in looks and temperament, and in their fierce love of Penelope. Siobhan had regarded Alice's intense love of her daughter as a blessing. She was able to continue working summers, while young Penny spent that time living with her aunt in the Cambridge house on

Rockingham Street, although not in the new garden-level flat recently carved out of what once was simply regarded as the basement. When Alice learned that Penny had applied to Boston University, she immediately set a crew to work, creating a private space for her favorite niece, her only niece. BU was literally a stone's throw across the Charles River from Alice's home, easy walking distance, and if Penny ended up not coming, she would simply rent the place out.

All those summers spent in Boston had contributed much to Penny's growth and maturation. Having grown up in rural New Mexico, her time in Boston did much to broaden her perspective. So much to absorb: the pace of life, the sheer density of people and places, the varieties of food and dress, the ocean and the beach, the smell of salt always in the air; and of course the ubiquitous monuments of New England history, so different from the old adobe churches of New Mexico, but both in the end sad testaments to the treatment of native peoples. And the metropolis itself, a hodgepodge of enclaves, each defined by a potpourri of race, ethnicity, religion, social and economic class — tensions between them simmering and hidden from view for the most part, still sometimes exploding in terrifyingly brutal ways, and then seemingly forgotten within the confines of Fenway Park. She sensed all this even as a little girl, learned how to safely navigate its conventions as an adolescent, but not until a student at CSF did she understand much of its causes and complexities.

But the time Penny spent alone with her aunt had been the most valuable. Early on, it became understood that their conversations would be privileged and confidential: what was said between them would stay between them. They talked of many things, but especially during Penny's middle and high school years, about sex and sexuality, gender roles and social expectations. Alice told her what it was like to grow up a lesbian in the 70s and 80s — lonely and isolated, ashamed of her feelings, wishing she was "normal." When she had finally confided in her younger sister, Siobhan had smiled and said, " Of course you're a lesbian, but thanks for telling me. You know, I love you dearly, as if you were my own sister." And they had both laughed at that, and hugged, and cried. It had been Siobhan who insisted that Alice apply to Mount Holyoke, a women's liberal arts college, where Alice flourished, intellectually, socially, and sexually. She knew that no man would ever be around to support her, that she would have to rely on herself. She had managed quite nicely, thank you very much, as she stood outside her Cambridge home, her dark red hair styled into submission, looking elegant, as always, in drawstring pants and a peasant blouse.

Not that much of a surprise, then, when Penny leapt from the back of the hired car, almost before it came to a stop at the curb, launched herself into Alice's welcoming arms, buried her face against her aunt's neck and quietly sobbed, "*Tía*, it's a man."

ΩΩΩ

Penny's eyes snapped open, instantly alert. Not frightened, not anxious really, intensely curious, as if the last few days were a dream from which she was finally waking, needing to anchor herself once more in reality. The light in the room was subdued. Turning her head to the right, a curtained window, filtering gray light — not yet dusk. She was in the bedroom of the garden-level flat, her new home. There was a desk and a bookshelf, already holding her books. Alice must have unpacked the belongings she had shipped ahead. Sure enough, her clock was resting on one of two twin nightstands, reading 3:05, not as late as she thought, unless it was still on Santa Fe time. Still, she must have slept most of the day; it would be Tuesday afternoon. She felt refreshed, her mind functioning, piecing things together. Not like when she had arrived, overwhelmed, having worked herself into a frenzied panic during the ride from Logan. The sight of her aunt smiling, that bright warm smile so like her mother's, had brought tears to her eyes, and she found herself flying into Alice's warm embrace, blubbering like a little girl. Her aunt, so calm and reassuring, had led her around back and put her to bed, knowing as always just what she needed.

The muted whistling of a tea kettle, quickly silenced — Alice making tea in the other room, no doubt. Penny smiled. Her aunt had promised that she would not wake up alone, and Alice always kept her word. Rousing herself to a sitting position, her eye caught movement at the doorless entry to the room. A reddish dog, a girl dog she was certain, padding tentatively over gray plush carpet toward the bed, her tail low and barely twitching, with flappy ears, a sweet face, and a questioning look in her eyes, as if asking permission. "It's ok, girl; come on," she beckoned. Bounding the remaining distance, and tall enough to lay her chin on the bed, she gazed longingly at Penny, who leaned forward and gently stroked her head.

"That's Sappho," Alice announced from the doorway, smiling. "She wanted to meet you."

"She's beautiful!" Penny declared, returning her aunt's smile, continuing to pet a very amenable Sappho.

"I found her at the shelter. I used to walk dogs there twice a week, for the exercise and to help out. Now I walk her twice a day," said with a loving chuckle and faux annoyance. "Take her for a walk and she'll be your friend for life, although I think she already is."

"Her coat is so soft... and such a pretty color."

"You would say that," Alice laughed. "She's the color of your hair. An Irish Setter mix. It's what first attracted me to her."

Penny giggled and, of course, blushed. Then, lecturing Sappho, "Do not let anyone ever call you a strawberry blonde!"

"Come, Sappho," Alice called. Let's give Penny some space to shower and dress. We'll wait for her in the other room." Sappho whimpered, gave Penny's hand a last lick, and reluctantly followed Alice out.

ΩΩΩ

"Feeling better?" Alice asked as Penny emerged 20 minutes later, freshly showered, hair washed and dried, wearing capris and a knit top.

"Much, thank you." Penny slid into the matching leather armchair across from her aunt. "Where's Sappho?" A coffee table stood between them, resting on a braided wool rug of muted reds and browns, defining the cozy sitting space opposite the kitchen and dining area.

"Out back, keeping the squirrels at bay. She's such a gentle soul, I can't imagine her doing one harm, but they tease her unmercifully. It's just the game they play, I suppose. Would you like some tea? It's lemon ginger," Alice offered, nodding toward the tea service on the coffee table and refilling her own cup.

"Please." Penny smiled at her aunt, taking a deep, cleansing breath. "Thank you so much, Aunt Alice, for this beautiful place, for taking care of me — you even organized all my stuff."

"Marisol helped with that — and honestly, dear, there wasn't much to put away."

"It will seem like a lot more in a week or two when it's scattered all over the floor." Penny giggled. "Who's Marisol?"

"She's Henry Rivera's cousin. You remember Mr. Rivera? He did odd jobs around here and my other properties. He's got his own crew now. They did all this — the excavation, the plumbing, the whole remodel. Anyway, Marisol lost everything in Hurricane Maria. Henry is her only family, and he took her in, but they really didn't have the room. I was looking for a new housekeeper, so she stays here now, in your old room. It's been good for me, having someone around, and she works miracles in the kitchen. I eat in most nights now. You can meet her this evening if you'd care to join us for dinner."

"I'd love to," said Penny, cocking her head, shrewdly assessing her aunt. "A new career, taking in strays — Sappho, Marisol, me."

"Well," Alice smiled, "I can afford to. Speaking of which..." she slapped down a credit card on the coffee table, "this is for you." She gave her niece a firm look that said she would brook no argument. Penny looked down at the card, her named embossed there, then again at her aunt, stunned, speechless. Alice continued. "This place belongs to you, for as long as you want it. Do whatever you like to make it your own; you do not need my permission. And you will charge all your bills and purchases to this card."

"I don't know what to say," Penny managed, barely above a whisper.

"Don't say anything. It's settled! Your mother and I have talked."

Penny laughed. "And she'll handle my father."

"As always. They will, however, continue to pay your phone bill, so that you will continue to call them — which I would hope you will do soon."

"I texted them on the way here from Logan, and I'll speak with them this evening. But Aunt Alice, you have already been so generous — I know you covered my tuition at CSF." Alice's turn to be speechless. "I'm good at math, remember? The numbers didn't add up."

"That was passing on in kind a good deed your mother once did for me, as you may well remember," said Alice, finding her voice. "And you should think of this in much the same way. I am delighted to have you here, all grown up, a college graduate following your dreams. You have filled a void in my life that I would have never known existed, had it not been for the generosity of your parents, sharing their daughter with me all those summers."

"But it's too much..."

"Not for me. These days I have more money than I know what to do with; I am always giving it away. And, especially in these dark days, it gives me great pleasure to help a strong, intelligent young woman pursue a doctorate. We women have to stick together, don't you think?" Just then Sappho barked at the French doors. Alice went to let her in, calling back over her shoulder, "Including this one."

Sappho bolted through the door, making what would have been a beeline for Penny if her paws had not been fighting for traction on the slick gray flooring, her nails clicking and clacking until finally finding purchase on the large oval rug. Penny fell to her knees to greet the charging dog, and much nose rubbing, scratching of ears, and slobbering kisses ensued.

Alice looked on, dumbfounded. "Honestly, I've never seen her react like this with anyone, not even me."

Penny looked up, grinning. "She must know I need a friend." And then to Sappho, "Ok girl, that's enough, for now. Your mistress and I are chatting." With that Penny resumed her seat, Sappho content to lie at her feet. "What kind of wood is that floor anyway? Reminds of the weathered cedar siding on the houses in Nantucket."

Alice, taking her seat again, after a quick pat of Sappho's head, "Very perceptive. But it's not wood; it's vinyl — Nantucket Harbor Vinyl Plank Flooring, to be precise. Quite lovely, isn't it? And so much easier to maintain."

"You don't trust me with genuine hardwood?" Penny smirked.

"Actually, all the furniture is solid oak, excepting the cushions, of course — sustainably grown, and handmade in Vermont, a small company started by a woman 10 or 12 years ago, I believe."

Penny sighed; there was so much to take in. "Mr. Rivera and his crew did a masterful job building this place, clearly, but the design and the decorating, that was you, *Tía*." Penny smiled at her aunt and saw a hint of a blush. "Maybe living here, I'll absorb some of your taste and elegant sensibility."

"Kind of you to say," said Alice, followed by a somewhat awkward pause. "That's twice you've called me *Tía*. I haven't heard that since you were 12."

Another sigh. "Maybe I'm feeling some of that same vulnerability. I do apologize for my hysterical behavior this morning."

"No need to apologize, dear. You know I won't press you, but I'm always available to listen."

Penny knew she would eventually tell her aunt everything; she had to tell someone, and there was no one she could trust more. Still, before she herself knew all the facts, she needed to be cautious. Say too much and she might even be putting her aunt at risk. Finally, she said, "Well, it's a man."

Alice laughed. "That much, I know."

Penny gave her a rueful smile. "It's just so damn complicated. His name is Michael. I've known him for about four years, but only quite recently did things get, you know, physical." She blushed. "And now, I think I may have fallen in love with him, and he might be feeling the same way, but he's off on some secret mission in Europe. I'm not to call or email — we really need to talk, and I'm just... frustrated. He will be coming here, to Boston, in a month or two, so he told me, but still...."

"May I ask whose idea it was to get, you know, physical?" Alice asked, gently probing but trying to keep the mood light.

That stopped her. She hadn't really thought about it that way. "I guess I did. I sort of insisted on it, actually."

"You had feelings you did not understand but wanted to. Perhaps now you do."

Stopped yet again. Her aunt, so insightful. "But I won't understand anything more until I see him."

"Well, until then, you can relax, settle in, walk Sappho," whose head lifted excitedly at the combination of those two words, "and have dinner with Marisol and me this evening."

Penny felt surprisingly lighter. She hadn't revealed too much and was rewarded with a new degree of clarity. She felt like hugging her aunt, so she did. "Oh, *Tía*, I think I'll call you that for the duration," she said, her face again pressed against her aunt's neck, but grinning this time.

"Please do."

CHAPTER 3

D inner was amazing. Marisol had prepared a traditional Puerto Rican dish, *Serenata de Bacalao*, a kind of cod salad. Desalted cod was something Penny had never heard of, but she devoured it with gusto, much to Marisol's delight. Penny's appreciation of the meal made up somewhat for her lame attempt to converse in Spanish, finally admitting that despite her upbringing in *Nuevo México*, she could really only claim the ability to nod and smile in Spanish. Languages were not her thing — unless they were dead, and therefore more amenable to her analytical prowess.

Marisol herself fascinated Penny. Late twenties and stunningly beautiful: flawless caramel skin, richly expressive dark eyes, straight black hair, tied back in a ponytail but probably reaching near her waist if set free. Despite a degree in environmental science, or perhaps because of it, she had lived alone in the mountains of Puerto Rico, supporting herself with the goats she raised and the produce she grew. Milk, homemade cheese, and organic vegetables supplied her with food and profit enough to live a comfortable if simple life. She missed that life, especially her goats. But despite her devastating loss, she was cheerful, energetic, and focused on the future. That future might include continuing her education. Apparently, the books she'd shelved below had tweaked her interest; she might ask to borrow a few. Her plan this evening, however, was to watch the Rivera children so that her cousin Henry and his wife Sarah could enjoy a rare night out together.

Lingering at the table with her aunt after Marisol's departure, with Sappho lurking beneath the table, Penny asked in her best imitation of nonchalance, "What exactly is your arrangement with Marisol?"

Alice laughed. "She's not my type, if that's what you're wondering."

"Not at all… ok, maybe a little." Penny smiled.

"Marisol is very smart, very independent, and very straight. Technically, she's employed by my management company as a housekeeper — let's leave it at that."

"Hiding something, *Tía*? Seems like you've a bit of Irish sheep rustler in your blood."

"Can't deny my own ancestry, now can I?" Alice smiled. "But I know what you're up to, my dear, alluding to that history. Always so curious. The truth is, your mother and I both admire our sheep rustling forebears, but for different reasons. Over time, that dispute, such as it was, became a way for us to acknowledge and tease each other about our different outlooks. A sort of private joke, I suppose."

That wasn't going to be enough to satisfy her niece, judging from the stony look on Penny's face. Sighing, Alice continued, "Siobhan has an affinity for the unconventional. She has always adored Thoreau, and she became fond of reciting Proudhon's dictum, 'property is theft,' once she encountered his work in college. She saw stealing sheep from the English aristocracy as a revolutionary act. Your mother, my sister, is a woman of high principle and grand dreams, and she does her best to live by her beliefs. No one can accuse her of being a spendthrift or a careless consumer. And judging by the dearth of your belongings, no one can accuse you of that either." Alice smiled at her niece. "But the world of Siobhan's dreams is not the one we live in, and to live in this one has often been a struggle for me, and I suspect for our Irish ancestors as well. I believe they stole those sheep simply to survive, at the cost of being cast from the ranks of respectable society. And yet, outcasts though they were, they found a way to create for themselves a worthwhile and meaningful life in this country. Something of that legacy is what I admire and embrace."

Penny reached out her hand, clasping and squeezing her aunt's. "Oh, *Tía*."

ΩΩΩ

Penny woke with the sun, rolled over, and slept for another three hours. When she finally stole up the backstairs, suppressing a desire to giggle, it must have been close to 9:00 a.m. She had been delighted to have found the backstairs intact and accessible from her new home. As a little girl, she had spent hours sneaking about, from the basement to the attic, unseen and unheard, and often popping out at the most awkward moments. Alice had shown her the folding doors flanking the kitchen counter of her flat the previous evening, behind which one might expect to find pantry shelves. Instead, a dimly lit passageway led to a half bath on one side, the laundry room on the other, and the narrow winding stairs straight ahead.

Reaching the landing off the main kitchen on the first floor, she spied Marisol rolling out dough. Slipping quietly into the room's center, Penny announced her presence with a casual, "Hi." Marisol responded with a full-body flinch and a muted scream. She turned, a rolling pin raised high, ready to ward off an imminent assault, to confront instead a smirking 22-year-old imp. Fear immediately morphed into annoyance and resolved into indulgence. "You get one pass, and that was it," said Marisol, brandishing the rolling pin, attempting but failing to sound like a high school principal.

"I'm sorry," said Penny, trying to contain her laughter and appear contrite. "I used to do that all the time when I was younger, and I just couldn't resist. Do you know about the backstairs?"

"I do the laundry, remember?" Marisol saw a shadow of shame or guilt cross Penny's face and sought quickly to lift it. "It is ok, really. We all need to remember what it feels like to be a child. May I fix you something to eat? Coffee?"

A hint of nausea at the thought of coffee. "I'm still full from last night, but some ginger tea might be nice. I can get it."

"It is no trouble," said Marisol, who was already filling the kettle. "You may eat anything you find here, anytime. I do not usually cook breakfast or lunch, but there are always fixings, fresh fruit, and baked goods, like the banana bread I see you have noticed. Please, slice as much as you like. Do not worry about using something up. I go to the market most days, and I am well practiced at making do with what is at hand. Dinners I do cook, and you are welcome to join us whenever you want."

As Marisol spoke, Penny snagged a mug, a teabag, and a plate, the last of which was soon covered with banana bread. She had set a place for herself at the table, just as the kettle whistled, and she was soon settled, dunking her tea bag with a spoon.

"I'd be a fool not to join you for dinner." Penny smiled. "But I do have a kitchen downstairs. I thought I would pick up some staples and stuff to nibble on. Maybe juice and bagels for breakfast, fruit or nuts for lunch. I'm not a big eater."

"That might change." Marisol's words hung in the air, not exactly an accusation, more an invitation.

"Why would you say that?" Penny's voice tentative, almost breaking.

Marisol took a seat around the corner from Penny's. "Herbal tea instead of coffee. No wine with dinner. Emotions near the surface."

"Is it that obvious?"

Marisol took Penny's hands in hers. "A woman with child has a look about her, some might say an aura. Even if it is very recent and the woman does not know herself."

"I was going to see a doctor in a week or so, have a test."

"That is wise. But you already know the result of the test, do you not? Still, it will be good to get a doctor's advice."

"Do you think my aunt knows?"

Marisol chuckled. "Of course, she knows. But she will allow you to tell her in your own time, when you are ready. She loves you very much. And she is so, so proud of you. *Su tía* is a remarkable woman."

"I'm beginning to understand that. Growing up, I spent my summers here. We always had a special relationship. But she was my aunt, and that's really all I saw." A cleansing breath. "Now I can appreciate her struggles as a woman, what she's had to overcome, all that she's accomplished. And how kind and sensitive and *knowing*. I am blessed to have her in my life, especially now."

"Believe me, Penelope, she is blessed to have you as well. Which reminds me, Alice will be away all morning, maybe all day, and she wanted me to ask you to take Sappho for a walk. She will do her business in the back yard if she must, but she much prefers the park along the river."

"Of course, I'll take her. I really must still be jet-lagged. I never thought to ask about *mi tía y la perrita*."

"Not to worry. They have already forgiven you."

ΩΩΩ

Sappho knew where she needed to go. Penny in tow, she took the most direct route to the pedestrian bridge fronting the Morris School, crossed above the highway, and down into Magazine Beach. Having relieved herself soon thereafter, she allowed Penny to take her on a more leisurely walk along the river. By midmorning, most of the joggers and dog walkers had come and gone, but the mild May weather had brought out a plethora of boats on the Charles: canoes and kayaks, small sailboats, even a scull or two. The sight of so much water and lush green grass seemed miraculous to Penny, having endured a persistent and worrisome drought during her four years in Santa Fe. The sight of sailboats tacking upstream in the light breeze completed the tranquil scene, a welcome respite from the tension and turmoil of the last few days. Then her cell phone buzzed. A text message had arrived, from Artemis, it read, and apprehension and anxiety returned with a vengeance.

Penny found a bench facing the river, Sappho at first content to lie in the grass at her feet. Then a cloud blocked the sun, the darkening waters of the river now portending an ominous current of inevitability. Sappho felt the change in mood and rose, sitting alert, a sentinel keeping watch, as Penny read the message, once, twice, and a third time. Its author claimed to be Michael's sister, with important information to convey from him, and proposed to meet face-to-face at a coffee shop on the Boston University campus that afternoon. Penny needed to scrutinize this text calmly and carefully before deciding what to do. She walked briskly toward the pedestrian bridge, Sappho trotting faithfully by her side, the leash slack, and together they walked off Penny's adrenaline rush on the quiet streets of the Cambridgeport neighborhood, altered but still familiar to her from summers past. Once home, they quenched their thirsts before turning to their respective tasks: Penny to her analysis, Sappho to her noontime nap.

Who was this Artemis, and could she be trusted? On the one hand, Michael had never mentioned having a sister. On the other hand, she seemed to know things that suggested a close relationship with him. She knew that Penny had the bronze Artemis; in fact, had instructed her to bring it to the meeting. More persuasive still was her knowledge that Michael had promised to return to Penny a certain blue article of clothing. Artemis had suggested a public place for the meeting, a coffee shop in the middle of a college campus. An odd choice for the execution of some nefarious act. And Penny could go there early to check it out. In fact, she needed to go to BU to get her student ID and email account. Two birds, one stone. Finally, the claim of having important information could be a ruse. Why not simply text or email it to Penny? Of course, electronic communications were less than secure these days, and Michael might not want to risk its exposure. On balance, Penny concluded, there would be little danger in heading to the campus, taking care of her student business, and staking out the coffee shop. She could always split if things felt sketchy. And she would have her Artemis close, and Michael's promise that she would keep her safe.

ΩΩΩ

Penny had an unobstructed view of the entrance to the coffee house from the small second-floor reading area of the BU bookstore next door. She had been sitting by the window for over an hour, the last 15 minutes watching the entrance carefully for an older woman — at least 50, given that Artemis claimed to be Michael's sister. True, Michael had never told Penny his actual age, hinting that it was probably greater than she imagined, but she figured at least 65. She had considered lowering that estimate based on Michael's performance in bed, but declined to do so after her research on the sex life of older men undertaken last evening before dinner. She'd read that it was not unusual for seventy-year-old men to father children, and that healthy men could have active sex lives well into their 80s and beyond. She'd embarked on that research project after loading Alice's Wi-Fi account into her phone, so she could call her parents. That call had been mercifully short; the one notable moment was when her mother mentioned again the dispute with her sister over the Irish sheep rustlers. Not a coincidence, Penny thought, and she had resolved then to discuss the matter with her aunt. That discussion had been accomplished. She was anxious to get this new mission underway.

The scheduled time for the meeting was fast approaching, with nary a sign of an older woman. Much earlier, Penny had checked out the coffee shop, Σαρια, the Greek name Artemis had texted, which she had found painted in blue over the door. It was a typical student hangout. Anyone over 30 would surely stand out, let alone a woman of 50 or more. She would give Artemis another five minutes. Fortunately, Penny had not wasted the time. To explain her lengthy presence in the bookstore, she had perused a book on Greek mythology, and in fact had learned a thing or two of curious interest if not import. Turns out that Artemis did have a brother, a twin brother, Apollo — and that the two of them were among a pantheon of only 12 genuine Olympian gods. There were many other immortals, of various ranks and status, but only 12 who carried the torch of Mt. Olympus, as it were. This Artemis would have never made the cut; she was late.

Entering Σαρια, Penny was immediately struck by the large framed photograph of a shallow bay of Mediterranean blue water, breaking gently on a white sand beach, backed by rugged hills. Not just stunning, but evocative. Of what — a memory, a longing? Something just out of reach.

"It's Saria."

"Excuse me?" uttered a distracted Penny, her eyes dropping from the photograph to the smiling fresh face of a young barista, with long curly black hair.

"The photograph you've been staring at. It's of the Greek island of Saria, the home of my family, and also the name of this shop."

"It's beautiful," said Penny, regaining her focus. "The Greek letters over the door?"

"In English, s-a-r-i-a, with the accent on the second syllable. Sa-rí-a." The barista smiled. "May I help you, Ms. Bauer?"

"Umm... how do you know my name?"

"Artemis told me to keep an eye out for you. She's running late. She apologizes and asks that you order whatever you want on her tab." She smiled and added, a co-conspirator, "I'd go for the baklava."

"So you know Artemis?" Penny felt herself relaxing.

"Oh, yes. She's a regular here." Bright smile. "I'm Cynna, by the way."

"Penny. Nice to meet you."

"Let me show you to the corner booth." Stepping behind the counter and leading the way. "And shall I bring you the baklava?"

"Of course." Penny giggled. "And some ginger tea, if you have it."

ΩΩΩ

The baklava was delicious. Sipping her tea and savoring the sweet flakey pastry, Penny scanned the room. Student types, their eyes down, focused on screens of one sort or another, no doubt connected to Saria's free Wi-Fi, mugs of cooling coffee at hand. Except for one guy, blonde and tanned, handsome in an obvious kind of way, looking out of place, as if central casting had made a mistake — and looking at her. Staring, and now standing, the arrogance of the smirk on his face matching the pace of his stride.

"That seat taken?" he asked, dripping smugness as he pointed to the bench seat around the corner from where Penny sat.

"As a matter of fact...."

"Come on, baby, move on over and let's get acquainted." He was making a move, clearly intending to push his way in next to her, when the flash of a bare arm crossed his chest, his knees buckled, and his body was twisted and smashed to the floor. Penny blinked, and there was Cynna, her knee planted in the center of his back, one hand pressing the side of his head roughly to the tile, her other hand pulling up his arm in an awkward position that his harsh moans suggested was quite painful.

"You fucking bitch," he growled through gritted teeth.

Cynna dug her knee in harder and jerked his arm, eliciting a sharp cry. "Now you've been rude to me as well as my guest. So... I'm going to start counting, and if you have not apologized to both of us before I get to 10, I'm going to break your arm."

"You wouldn't do that."

Cynna laughed at that and began counting. "One... two... three..."

"Ok... ok! I'm sorry, alright?"

"And what are you sorry for?" Another jerk of the arm, another cry.

"For being rude to you and your friend."

"Very well. Here's what's going to happen now. I'm going to stand you up and walk you to the door. But the next time you come in here, you will leave without your balls."

As Cynna pushed him out the door, she was treated to a spontaneous round of applause from the shop's patrons, men and women alike. Acknowledging the tribute with a shy smile and a deep blush, she dusted off her hands and retreated to her spot behind the counter.

Penny had little time to absorb, let alone process, what had just happened, for a harried woman in a flight attendant's uniform had rushed through the door and was making straight for Penny's booth. Sucking air as if she'd run a 100-meter sprint in heels, she extended her hand. "Penelope? I'm Artemis. Sorry I'm late."

Penny took her hand, more a quick squeeze than a shake, scrutinizing her familiar-looking face. "Have we met before?"

Waving Penny over to make room for her to sit, Artemis snapped, "Everybody asks me that. I look like Tina Fey, ok? At least when she was younger."

"And what would Ms. Fey like to order this afternoon," playfully asked Cynna, who had followed in her wake.

Artemis laughed, her annoyance forgotten. "An Americano, with a double shot. I've got the redeye to London tonight."

"Very good," Cynna replied, with a sly wink at Penny. "But why did you tell me that Penelope was a strawberry blonde? Anyone can see that she's a redhead."

Penny narrowed her eyes at Artemis, who sighed, "Not helpful, Cynna." But the barista had already scurried away, giggling.

"So... you know I dislike being called a blonde," Penny said, her tone a bit chilly.

"Yes." A deep breath. "I know everything about you. I know you had a promising future as a competitive skier until you twisted a knee when you were 12. I know you were a striker on your high school soccer team and voted captain your senior year. I know you were the college valedictorian and that you were invited to give the student speech at the alternative graduation. You declined that invitation, telling the student organizers that one of their own should give that speech. Shall I go on?"

Penny sat stunned. "How? Why?"

"That is a long story best told to you by Michael, who should be here sometime next week. His meetings have gone well, better than we had hoped, but there are still risks to be discussed."

Cynna returned just then, carefully placing the steaming coffee cup on the table, as Artemis scowled, but unconvincingly. "Will that be all?" Cynna asked with a coy smile.

"Yes, thank you," said Artemis, all business now. "Anything to report?"

"Nothing significant. There was a small incident with a would-be suitor before you arrived."

"I could have handled him," Penelope interjected, perhaps a bit accusingly.

Cynna nodded. "I'm certain you could have. But my place, my rules, my responsibility."

"I gather we won't be seeing him again," said Artemis.

"Not likely," Cynna replied. "I only had to count to three."

As Cynna departed, Artemis turned to Penny. "You mustn't be too hard on Cynna. She was just doing her job."

"Her job?"

"To protect you. The truth is, there are roughly 100 young women just like her who would gladly sacrifice their lives to keep you safe."

"What?" Penny again sat stunned. "This is about the baby, isn't it?"

Artemis smiled. "Michael told me you would have figured that out. Which reminds me..." She pulled a business card from her purse and handed it to Penny. "Helena Zoya, board-certified OBGYN. Call and make an appointment or just show up. She'll make time for you. She's one of us."

"Who the hell is us?" Penny wailed, loud enough to draw the looks of a few patrons in the front. She reined in her frustration and confusion — whatever the range of feelings fueling her Irish temper — at least enough to state the obvious more quietly. "I seem to be the only one here who doesn't know what's going on."

"Michael should really be the one to tell you the whole story. Besides, I have to leave for Logan shortly. But I'll do my best to answer your questions."

Penny squared her shoulders, channeling the trial attorney her father always imagined her to be. "Let's start with you. You say you're Michael's sister, but you can't be much over 40."

"Forty! Do I really look that old? Oh, never mind. Yes, I am his sister, his twin, actually."

That produced a sardonic laugh, but subdued enough not to draw attention. "Next you're going to tell me that he's Apollo and the two of you are Olympian gods."

Artemis chuckled. "I hadn't intended to, but now that you mention it. Ever wonder what the 'A' stood for in A. Michael Ambros? But we prefer the term immortals."

"You can't expect me to believe that," Penny replied, nonplussed.

"No, but it would make things a hell of a lot easier." A sigh. "You and your child are in danger because she too will be immortal. But until she is born, she's vulnerable."

"She?"

"She is destined to become Queen of the Amazons," said Artemis, beaming with a pride she knew would soon be Penny's. "Cynna and Dr. Zoya are two of the 100 or so remaining Amazons, who have struggled to endure without a queen for three millennia. Their race won't survive much longer without a queen." A quick look at her watch and Artemis took Penny's hand in both of hers. "You must listen carefully now; there's not much time. Believe what you will, but hear me out."

Penny simply nodded, too bewildered to speak, let alone continue her cross-examination.

"My brother has convinced the Olympian Council to sanction the birth of your child, forbidding any immortal from attempting to thwart it. But that command means little to Aphrodite, who is — how can I put this politely — a narcissistic bitch. Unfortunately, she is quite an accomplished seductress and can secure unwitting assistance from just about anyone. She poses a real danger to you and possibly to those you love.

"We have Amazons watching you, your parents, and your aunt. You will not see them, but they are close, and should you feel in danger at any time, you can summon them by pressing the red panic button on this key chain," which she pulled from her purse and handed to Penny.

"Can I press it now?" A small smile, humor being Penny's coping mechanism of last resort.

Artemis chuckled, understanding the strength of character that quip revealed. "Did you bring the bronze Artemis?" Penny drew the statuette from her backpack, handing her to the living Artemis, who stroked her lovingly. "She was forged for me by Hephaestus many years ago. A story for another day. But she will protect you, as Michael promised.

"The bronze has special sensitivity to certain types of emotional energy and transmits that energy directly to my brain. Human emotions, unless extremely intense, don't register at all. But the energy of immortals always does. If an immortal comes close to my bronze namesake, I will know, and I also see colors that reveal the nature of his or her feelings — red for malevolence, white for erotic passion, and so forth. Let me tell you, Penelope, my brain was lit up something fierce last Sunday night. I couldn't sleep. But then again, neither did you."

Artemis smirked; Penny blushed.

"So... keep this Artemis on your dining table," handing the statuette back to Penny. "If Didi comes close, I'll know."

"Didi?"

"The immortal bitch."

CHAPTER 4

Eleven days had passed since Penny's meeting with Artemis, and according to the latter, there was a slim chance Michael would arrive sometime this evening. It was a warm, sunny Spring day. Penny, in shorts and a tank top, was sitting with Sappho on the covered front porch of the Cambridge Victorian, trying to tame the maelstrom of feelings threatening to overwhelm her. She had provisionally accepted the truth of what Artemis had told her, having been unable to construct a plausible explanation for what would otherwise have to be an elaborate deception, with no discernible purpose. Her conversation with Dr. Zoya, who had confirmed her pregnancy, reinforced that view.

Helena Zoya, at first sight, had looked surprisingly young for an M.D. To Penny's eye, she and Cynna, the barista, could have been twins. Helena, as she had encouraged Penny to call her, had explained that she and Cynna were indeed sisters. In fact, she told her, all the Amazons were sisters or half-sisters, owing to a common father — the god Ares — and one of five mothers. The Amazons were organized like a beehive; only the queens could reproduce, the rest of them were sterile. Yes, she appreciated the irony of her chosen profession. Helena and Cynna were daughters of Hippolyta, one of the twin queens who were both killed at Troy. Yes, Amazons could be killed, but they did not die of natural causes, as their bodies stopped aging at 25. During the reign of Penthesilea and Hippolyta, the number of Amazons had increased to just over 1,000. Since their deaths, the strength of the hive had been considerably diminished, in both number and direction. Thus, the importance of the child Penny carried. Helena told her of the ancient prophecy, delivered by the Oracle at Delphi and recorded there, that the Amazons would remain without a queen until such time that the god Apollo, through intercourse with a mortal woman of high character, would produce a daughter to be born immortal, and destined to assume the mantle of queen, but only insofar as he renounce for all time his right and claim to immortality. Since that conversation two days prior, Penny had been struggling with her anger at being used for a purpose not of her choosing, and her wonder at the extraordinary sacrifice Michael had apparently made.

Sappho raised her head and issued a soft bark, distracting Penny momentarily from these thoughts. Just another plug of baseball fans on the sidewalk, heading for Fenway, less than a mile from where they sat. The Red Sox were at home for a Sunday doubleheader scheduled for a 2 p.m. start, but it was not yet noon. Penny had been reliably informed earlier that the beer was just as cold during batting practice.

Sappho had a well-calibrated repertoire of responses to strangers. Her soft bark, what Alice called a "boof," was a casual notice of approach. A sharp bark raised the level of alert when, for example, someone was at the gate or the door. At that point, Sappho's nose would be in the air, scent being her method of threat assessment. If she smelled no threat, her reaction would range from a whimpering submissiveness with those from whom prior acquaintance guaranteed a warm greeting or even a treat, to something more dignified and reserved. A low growl, on the other hand, meant trouble — Sappho poised to attack at the least provocation.

Penny had heard Sappho growl only once, when a man claiming to be from the Cambridge Zoning Authority came to the door, asking about the recent renovations. Being a realtor, Alice was quick to recognize the ruse, insisting that the man produce his official credentials. He had stammered some sort of excuse and quickly departed. Suspecting that the inquiry might concern her, Penny texted her suspicions to Artemis. It seemed that the Amazons watching the house had already confronted the man, questioned him, and convinced him to take a vacation in Maine. They had only had to count to three to get him on the bus.

Just then, Sappho leaped to her feet, charging down the stairs and toward a young man dressed in black, who had opened the gate and was kneeling down to receive the charging dog. At which point, much nose rubbing, scratching of ears, and slobbering kisses ensued. Penny experienced a feeling of déjà vu, the vision of Sappho running to her over the vinyl flooring in the garden flat passing before her eyes. Finally standing, she called out, challenging the intruder, "Who are you?"

The man stood, one hand resting still on Sappho's head, as the dog sniffed at the front pocket of his black jeans. "Hello, Penelope," he said, smiling sweetly.

His face was familiar, shaggy black hair, a black T-shirt under a stylishly thin black leather jacket — a look that suggested a bad boy from the wrong side of the tracks. "Do I know you?" A slight crack in her voice, which did not go unnoticed by either of them.

"Rather intimately," he replied, pulling from his front pocket some lacy blue panties. "I believe these are yours."

Penny gasped, a hand flying to cover her mouth. "Michael?"

Approaching her now, Sappho trotting lovingly at his side. "Yes... and no. I'm Michael Kalomoira now, 23 years old, and aging as we speak." Standing at the bottom of the stairs, he sniffed the panties and tossed them up to her. "Shall I show you my passport?"

Catching the panties and examining them, she giggled and blushed, despite herself. "I can't believe you did that."

"I bet there's a lot you still can't quite believe." Tenderness in his eyes as he gazed up at her. "Are you going to invite me in, or shall we talk on the porch?"

"I think you broke Sappho," she said.

He laughed. "I just have a way with redheads."

ΩΩΩ

They had at least four hours before they would have to head upstairs for dinner. Penny had brewed some lemon ginger tea, and they were sitting in her flat across the coffee table from each other, in the matching leather armchairs. Michael had shed his jacket. Penny was still in her shorts and tank top, although she felt naked under Michael's intense gaze. She had made him wait on the porch while she ushered Sappho reluctantly inside and called out to her aunt. Penny told her of Michael's early arrival, and how he had apparently charmed her dog beyond all measure. Alice narrowed her eyes at Sappho, who seemed to cover her chagrined face with her front paws as she lay at their feet. As they spoke, Penny could feel her anger mounting. She wanted her aunt to meet Michael, but she needed to get answers to some hard questions first. They had decided that dinner would be a group affair, assuming Penny hadn't sent him packing by then. Face to face now, it was time for the truth. No more secrets.

Michael spoke first. "Do you believe that I am the father of the child you carry?"

She nodded. It was all she could do, staring at this man who was and wasn't the man she had fallen in love with, wanting to scream at him and pound his chest, but also wanting to feel him pressed against her, inside her. Simply to contain that conflict demanded all her strength.

"Can I then assume you've decided to grant the reality of Olympian immortals and Amazons?"

Another nod and a resigned sigh. "It's either that, or I'm trapped in the Matrix."

Michael smiled. "Ok, then. From the beginning. There's an ancient prophecy..."

"I know about that. Helena... Dr. Zoya told me about it a few days ago."

"Good. It's good you've seen the doctor."

"Don't you trust me?" she hissed, the venom in her voice surprising her and clearly wounding him.

"Penelope..." he implored, his eyes tearing, choking them back. "I trust you with my life. You are my life."

That stopped her. What could she say to that? Shocked at the depth of her anger, pained at the hurt her words had caused. Fighting back her own tears.

"I know you're angry," he said. "You have every right to be. You feel used."

Exactly! That's exactly how she felt. That was at the root of things, the root of her anger and her feelings of betrayal. If she could hold onto that, focus on that, maybe she could get past it. That was her hope, her desperate hope. "Yes. I do."

Michael took a deep breath, exhaled. Never had he felt so vulnerable. Everything depended on what he said now. All he could do was tell the truth and hope the truth was enough. "I'll admit that when I first met you, I thought you might very well be the woman of high character the prophecy foresaw. Artemis investigated, and everything she found — truthfully, it all fit. But my attitude toward you changed almost immediately. You became my student — an extremely intelligent young woman, courageous, inventive, a joy to teach. And then I had to struggle to hold onto that view of you because something much deeper called to me—a siren's call. You told me that you felt desired — your words. But for me, it was more than that. I fell in love with you. And then your toast. You believed we were on an equal footing, but you didn't know then about the prophecy. My hesitation was about my fear that you would feel exactly as you do now. But you were so determined." Recalling her insistence, her bold resolve, he chuckled. "Not that I'm putting this on you. I could have said no, I could have left... at least, before you kissed me." He paused, his mind seized by a sudden realization. "I think that had I slept with you simply to fulfill the prophecy, you would not have conceived. Fate knowingly brought us together, the cosmic matchmaker, the clever Mistress of Destiny. She knew we'd fall in love and that our love would overpower the science of contraception to create this child."

He looked at her expectantly, saw that she was considering what he'd said, her eyes turned inward. Often, he imagined her mind as a finely tuned Swiss watch, the gears patiently turning, things gently falling into place. Only when all was weighed and brought into balance would she speak. Finally, she lifted her eyes to his, a last test of the verdict she had reached. "I'm still mad at you, " she said, her shoulders relaxing, a faint grin gracing her lovely face, already aglow with the new life growing inside her.

Michael wanted to leap over the table and pull her into his arms, but it was too soon for that. Instead, he just smiled and said, "I can live with that."

"Is it true you're no longer a god?" she asked.

"I was never a 'god,' at least not in the sense you are probably imagining. I couldn't actually alter events or get someone to do something he or she didn't really want to do."

"But three weeks ago, you were an old man."

"Appearances can be deceiving."

"This is not the time to be cute."

"You're right," Michael conceded. "The man you knew as Professor Ambros was me, in all essential respects except appearance. I was your teacher then, and I did my best for you in that role. This might surprise you, if that is still possible, but when Professor Ambros looked in a mirror, he saw the man seated across from you. What you, and those around you saw, was what you wanted to see, what you expected to see. As an Olympian, I could tap into the unconscious archetypical structure common to a time and culture and project an image. Consider it something like mass hypnosis. And I had access to the documents and accoutrements necessary to support that projection. Olympians are master illusionists and forgers, or if you prefer, con men and women. With one notable exception, and a few minor lapses and indiscretions, the immortals of Mt. Olympus have used this power to advance the truth and to promote justice. The other power I had, which Artemis and the other immortals still do, is to read energy — auras, if you will." Michael could not resist a little smirk. "I think my sister already explained this to you."

"She did." Penny blushed. "Actually, I wanted to ask you about that, because I saw light that night too, when it should have been pitch black."

"It *was* pitch black," he said, remembering: all his senses alive save sight; blind and yet seeing it all unfolding. A shake of his head to clear it. "Tell me exactly what you saw?"

"Well, when you first... um...." Penny blushed. "When you first entered me, I saw, or rather felt a flash of blinding light, like the lightning you see with your eyes closed. But then, there was soft white light swirling all around, not enough to see anything clearly. It was... comforting, enveloping."

Michael smiled. "That was me. You were reading me. Remarkable!" He paused, marshaling his thoughts. "I know you trust your mind, and rightly so. I envy your intelligence. But sometimes analysis needs to give way to intuition. You have an ability, apparently, that I had thought reserved to the immortals. Granted, there were special circumstances, but you should listen to your gut, as they say. Trust your reason, yes, but trust your intuition too, and if the two conflict, I would choose the latter."

Penny was warmed by his praise, and yet, she felt like Michael's student again and was not entirely comfortable with that. "Thank you, Professor," she said, a little sardonically.

"I thought we had agreed that I was no longer your teacher. In fact, I believe that we have been teaching each other from the very beginning. I have learned as much if not more from you than you from me."

Penny sighed. She could believe, perhaps, that her analytical skills were sharper than his, but Michael was the unsurpassed champion of rhetoric. "Be that as it may," she said in her best professorial voice, "I gather from what you have told me that you are, in fact, no longer an immortal, if I may be permitted to correct my earlier use of the inappropriate term, god."

Michael laughed. A genuine hearty laugh. Penny had come back to him, smart mouth and all. "Do I really sound like that?" Penny shrugged her shoulders and smirked, feeling too as if they had arrived at some kind of equilibrium. "Yes, to answer your question, I am no longer immortal, just your humble mortal servant, or maybe not so humble."

"And you knew that was a real possibility when we... um"

"Yes."

"It was a lot to give up," she said.

"Not at all," he replied tenderly. "Recall that moment in the Odyssey, when Circe offers Odysseus immortality and the promise of unlimited hot sex? He turns her down. Remember why?"

"Penelope," she said

"Smart man, Odysseus."

ΩΩΩ

That had made her cry. Not a soft trickle of a ladylike tear or two down her cheek. More like a flood. She'd been on an emotional rollercoaster for two weeks, and she needed a good cry. She was wiping her nose with her bare arm as Michael searched the flat for tissues. He found some in the bedroom, dropping the box on the coffee table as he raced to the French doors, where Sappho was scratching frantically, her leash draped in her mouth. Clearly a conspiracy was afoot, but it seemed a good one. So, after Penny composed herself, splashing her face briefly at the kitchen sink, and downing a glass of water, the three of them went for a walk.

As they walked, they talked. Michael used the time to supply Penny with the history of the seemingly inevitable current in which they now found themselves immersed. The Olympians all knew about the ancient prophecy, he told her, but they didn't give it much thought. What difference would it make if the Amazons got a new queen, given the belief shared by most of the Olympians that it's only a matter of time before human beings destroy themselves if not the entire planet?

"Artemis and I saw things differently. The problem at its root was the increasingly prevalent vision of the good life as acquisitive. If you are what you own, the more you own, the more you are. It's a simple equation, but one that ultimately ends in self-destruction — of the individual, the community, the earth itself. The antidote, we believed, was to reinvigorate the classical vision of the good life, the ethical life, the life enriched by the pursuit of truth and justice. And in this, the Amazons could play an important role. The myths and stories of Amazons contrived by mortal poets focus on their martial prowess, missing the crucial fact that they fight only in defense — and specifically, defense of the Olympian values, the core of which is the classical vision of the good life. Thus, an organized community of Amazon warriors, strategically directed, could be a powerful force in the battle against acquisitiveness."

This much, he told her, they presented to the Olympian Council years ago, to revive interest in the ancient prophecy, and to seek support for their efforts to develop a strategy for the training and deployment of a renewed Amazon army. "Off we went, me to the College of St. Frances, where I found a genuine longing among young students like you for the ethical life, and Artemis to the scattered cells of remaining Amazons, holding out the chance that their queen could be restored. The mere possibility was energizing, and Artemis encouraged and directed them to seek the weapons of the twenty-first century. Our army of Amazons will be composed of the most sophisticated cyber warriors the world has ever seen. And with a queen to unify and guide them, their collective power, the power of the hive, will increase exponentially."

"I think I know where this is going," said Penny. "Liberal arts education."

"Exactly! We are going to bankroll liberal arts colleges, not just here, but around the world, first with the ill-gotten gains of organizations like Kinslaw, and later with the profits of corporate capital."

"You mean, you're going to steal their money." A statement, not a question.

"I think your mother would say we're going to liberate their money." Michael smiled. "The people who run these corporations are ruining lives and killing the planet. Should we sit back and allow them to do that?"

Penny sighed. "I'm not prepared to argue the point right now. What I want to know is why you didn't tell me all this before you abandoned me on Monday morning. Left me on my own to realize at 30,000 feet that I was pregnant, and that...." She snorted.

"That what?"

"That I'm in love with you." She stopped walking, turned to face him, glaring, and all but shouted. "I love you, ok? But I'm still pissed!"

Michael beamed. A reaction he knew would only fuel her fit of pique, but he didn't care. She loved him! Not that he harbored serious doubt about her love, but hearing it from her lips for the first time gave him such a rush. He imagined himself, standing atop the summit of Mt. Olympus, proclaiming his joy to the whole world. But as he came down the slope to the present moment, he confronted Penny's scowl, and if he wasn't mistaken, Sappho's as well. He needed to say something. Tentatively, he asked, "If I had told you then, would you have believed me?"

"We'll never know," she snapped. "You didn't give me the chance."

He couldn't argue with that. "Fair enough," he said, searching for the truth he owed her, a truth he hadn't yet admitted to himself. "I guess I was afraid."

"Afraid of what?"

He gazed into her eyes, emerald in the bright sunlight, sparkling with flecks of gold. "Afraid of losing you."

She held his gaze and looked into his soul. The last of his facade was crumbling; he was utterly sincere. No longer a god, no longer hiding in illusions. Just a man, a man in love with her, admitting his greatest fear, his fear of losing her. She could turn and walk away and totally destroy him. Acknowledging that power chilled her. She wouldn't turn away — she couldn't — but she was not yet prepared to move forward either. There could be no more secrets between them; she willed him to continue, and he did.

"I should have told you. You had a right to know the twists of Fate that had transformed our unbridled night of passion into so much more. I did feel the need to keep you safe, and what I said to you, and my trip to Greece, was to assure that. But even then, I knew deep down that I was rationalizing. I'm sorry."

A silence stretched between them, broken by Sappho's bark. Both of them quickly scanned the surrounding neighborhood but saw nothing unusual and no one close. Penny looked down at Sappho, perplexed. The dog was staring back at her, wide-eyed, twitching her head in Michael's direction. "Ok, girl. I get the message." Penny leaned toward Michael, softly kissed his cheek, and spoke to him, quietly but firmly. "You will never keep anything from me again."

Michael did not respond. He didn't have to, for she had spoken a simple truth. They walked home without speaking, companionably, both processing, each in their own way, what had transpired between them. Sappho had an extra bounce in her step and a self-satisfied grin on her face.

They arrived back at her flat, an hour or so still to dinner. Penny felt drained — drained and sweaty. "I'm going to take a shower," she said.

"Can I join you?" Michael asked with a salacious grin.

"I don't think that's a good idea. We still have things to discuss." But his question prompted her to notice that Michael had no luggage. "Where's your stuff?"

"With the Amazons. I didn't want to presume."

That pleased her. That he respected her space. "Well, it's a big bed. Sappho can sleep between us." She smiled sweetly at him, turned, and disappeared into the bedroom.

ΩΩΩ

Apparently they'd been thinking the same thing, Penny in the shower, Michael in a leather chair watching the sun dropping in the west. They had to decide what to tell Alice, and quickly — the dinner hour was fast approaching. Fortunately, Penny had not revealed too much, and nothing that to Michael's mind could not be easily explained. Both agreed that Penny should not actively lie to her aunt, just withhold certain facts. After all, they need only hide the more fantastic elements of their story, and, as Michael pointed out, he was quite adept at disguising the truth. Penny insisted on revealing her pregnancy; besides, Marisol already knew and suspected that Alice did as well. That was their plan, such as it was, as they headed up the back stairs.

The savory aroma hit them first as they reached the first-floor landing and entered the kitchen. Marisol was just finishing up and spotted them right away. "Michael, this is Marisol — environmental scientist, entrepreneur, and chef extraordinaire."

Marisol wiped her hands on her apron, reached out to shake Michael's. "Penny is too kind. I am just a poor country girl from the mountains of Puerto Rico. Nice to meet you." She smiled.

"Well," said Michael, "something smells delicious." Inhaling deeply and smiling broadly, to make his point.

"The *sofrito*, the sauce for a simple rice dish from my home, *arroz con gandules*."

Penny winked at Marisol. "Perhaps you could give Michael lessons in humility and cooking. He could benefit from both."

"I can cook," he replied, to everyone's delight.

"Please go through," said Marisol, repressing her laughter. "Alice is waiting there. I will bring the food in a moment."

Michael followed Penny into the dining room, then strode purposefully to where Alice was sitting, extending his hand as she rose. "Michael Kalomoira," he said. They shook, she replied, "Alice O'Connor."

"O'Connor — patron of warriors."

Alice gestured for them to sit as Marisol placed the casserole on the table. "You know your Gaelic history?"

"Let's just say I have an interest in the family," he said, sitting next to Penny and squeezing her hand. "Thank you for your hospitality, Ms. O'Connor," he continued. "You have a beautiful home, and I might add, a beautiful niece."

Alice chuckled. "Alice, please. And compliments for the two of us in one breath. I'm betting that Marisol received hers in the kitchen.

"As a matter of fact..." Marisol giggled.

Michael warmed to Alice immediately. "Some might think you a bit... cynical, Alice."

"Let's just say I am a woman of the world."

"Touché."

Conversation continued in this playful vein, as they served themselves until Alice asked Michael, "Would you like some wine?"

"No, thank you," he replied. "Not for another eight and a half months."

Penny groaned and narrowed her eyes at him. "This is Michael's way of letting the tiny elephant in the room out of the bag." Another scowl at him. "We are going to have a baby in, yes, eight and a half months." Penny looked to her aunt and saw nothing but love in her eyes.

"If I may, how do you feel about this, Penelope?" Alice asked gently.

Penny gave her aunt a rueful smile. "I feel shocked, dismayed, and pissed at the manufacturers of birth control pills. And I feel scared... but also excited and, yes... happy." Michael beamed, leaned in, and tenderly kissed her cheek.

Alice smiled and raised her glass. "Well then, congratulations!" Taking a healthy sip, she added, "And I won't be giving this up."

"Not to derail the celebratory mood," said Michael, "but Penny's pregnancy raises complications of which you need to be aware." Alice and Marisol sat bemused, but he had their attention. "My sister and I own and operate a private security firm. We are currently developing some powerful cyber security software that, should it fall into the wrong hands, could prove quite devastating. I was in Greece discussing our own security arrangements with the powers supporting our work — Western powers, be assured. As part of the plan we devised, my sister Artemis, who manages the personal protection and surveillance part of our business, has assigned some of her people to watch over Penny's parents and all of us as a precautionary measure. I think you can understand why."

"Young women, athletic, most of them with dark curly hair?" asked Alice

"Yes. She calls them her Amazons. You spotted them?"

"Marisol did. Don't worry. I doubt anyone else would have noticed. I did manage to get Sappho close enough to give them a good sniff. She gave them a clean bill of health, but I'm wondering now if I can trust her judgment, after the way you charmed her." The dog, in her usual spot beneath the table, whimpered.

Michael laughed. "Don't be too hard on Sappho. To her, I probably smelled of Penny, as if I were, say, an article of her clothing." Penny blushed and lowered her head to hide her grin. Michael turned to Marisol. "May I ask how you knew?"

"I have brown skin and I speak Spanish. That is enough to make me a criminal in today's America. No matter that I am a U.S. citizen. I have been stopped and questioned by federal, state, and even Cambridge authorities. I carry my passport everywhere I go now, just to avoid the hassle. I am afraid that one time I will be stopped, and they will keep my passport or tear it up. Like Nazi Germany. Next they will be loading me on a train. So, of necessity, I have developed keen observation skills, especially for spotting those who watch."

Penny rubbed her belly protectively. She felt ashamed to be an American. Something had to be done. Michael had a plan for the people who were ruining lives and destroying the planet: make them pay, literally, and turn their money against the destructive values they promote. She had no need to debate the point with Michael. Marisol had made the argument for him.

ΩΩΩ

Dinner conversation after that was subdued — pleasant, but subdued. The food, of course, was delicious. Penny, whose concern for Marisol had stolen her appetite, ate far more than anyone, despite herself. When finally they descended the back stairs, Sappho leading the way, they were greeted by Michael's bags resting just inside the French doors.

"Your stuff," she said, checking the doors, both locked. "Do the Amazons have a key?"

"Something like that," Michael grinned.

"Will they protect Marisol if, you know, ICE or some other assholes confront her again?"

"There are protocols in place. Trust me, they will give their lives to keep her safe."

"And this is all about our baby," said Penny, troubled. "It seems so... extreme."

"Like a beehive, Penelope. They will do anything to protect their queen."

Penny plopped into one of the leather armchairs, absently stroking Sappho's head, the dog sitting beside her. "Will our daughter have a choice? It seems she already belongs to the Amazons."

Michael heard the genuine concern in her voice. He took up a spot on the rug in front of her. Sappho shifted a bit so he could pet her too, and he complied. "Of course she will. No one will force her to assume the throne, as it were. The Amazons will treat her with respect, reverence even, and they will watch over her. But they will ask nothing of her. I must warn you though." He smiled. "She will have your intelligence and your courage. She will want to know everything and do everything. And there is always Fate to reckon with."

"And what will she get from you?" she asked, her heart a little lighter.

"My charm and good looks, of course." He laid a hand upon her knee, letting his fingers walk slowly north.

Penny shook her head. "I can't do this, not yet."

Michael's fingers retraced their steps at the same slow pace. "So Sappho sleeps between us?"

"Tonight at least. Then we'll see."

Penny brushed her teeth and climbed into bed with the dog and her thoughts, while Michael took a long-overdue shower. The room was illuminated by the filtered light of a full moon, or one nearly so, and the bright strip escaping under the door to the bathroom. Two weeks ago, in the darkening twilight, she had raised a glass of champagne in an innocent toast — well, not so innocent, perhaps. All that had happened since was unimaginable, beyond belief — and yet, she felt safe with Sappho in the bed in her aunt's basement, waiting for the man she loved to join them. Her fear of the future was receding. She was beginning to see more clearly the path ahead, and for the first time since that fateful Sunday night, she felt a measure of contentment, even happiness.

Michael emerged from the bathroom, vigorously toweling his hair, his body a backlit silhouette in boxer shorts. It was her first real look at his physique. She had felt it, explored it, but those perceptions had been clouded by illusions of age. He wasn't old now. Toned without being muscled, slim without being skinny, classically sculptured, balanced like a fine wine. Her eyes lingered rather too obviously at the region of his shorts, and she felt the pull, the longing of *eros*, which she attempted to mask with a question. "How do you know you're 23?"

Michael grinned at her. He didn't need his immortal powers to read what was on her mind. But he had no intention of pressing the moment just now. "That's what it says on my passport. I couldn't very well have put 3,534, now could I? All I know for certain is that my body is older today than it was yesterday, and that for me is a totally new experience." He hung the towel, finger-combed his hair, flipped off the light, and slipped into the bed. Nuzzled comfortably between them, Sappho sighed, as if she had died and gone to heaven.

"So you just picked 23, arbitrarily?" Penny asked.

"I know you have a thing for older men."

That made her giggle. "When's your birthday?"

"Jeez... sometime in October, I think. I should really know these things. I was in such a rush to get here."

"You're right, you know," she said, basking in the glow of his last remark.

"About what?"

"The money. You're right. My mother is right. The masters of capital are the real monsters, the real criminals. Marisol convinced me. Take their money; let me help you."

It was Michael's turn to savor her words. "I have to go back to the Island soon. I want you to come with me."

"The Island?"

"Saria. Last stronghold of the Amazons and home to Mt. Olympus Security, LLC. You have a few months before classes begin."

"Oh, God! What am I going to do about school?"

"Don't think about that now. Think about a secluded white sand beach, the gentle surf of the South Aegean Sea. Think about sharing that place with Alice and Marisol, your parents, and even Sappho. Everyone could see what we are building there, even if we can't tell them exactly what we intend to do. The Amazons would treat us all like royalty.

"I can picture you stepping from the small sailboat grounded in the sand, bare feet splashing through the last of the receding tide as you approach the assembled guests. Your gown, a simple but elegant muslin dress, flowers in your hair, matching the bouquet you carry in your hands."

"Please don't tell me you are asking me to marry you."

"No need to ask. We both know we are already bound together irrevocably. I am asking you to come with me to Saria and think about how nice it would be to share with those we love the reality and the beauty of our union."

Penny was searching for a witty response, but there was too much truth in what he said. She hadn't really thought about marriage — she'd had a few other things on her mind. But as she considered it now, it did seem like a done deal. They loved each other deeply, and they had consecrated that love in a manner unmatched in human history, or immortal history for that matter. It was not simply the fact that she was pregnant; the growing child they had created against all odds was proof that Fate had ordained their union. A celebration was indeed in order. "Ok," she finally said, "I'll think about it."

"What do you think, Sappho?" he asked the dog, as he scratched behind her ears. "I've been waiting over three and a half millennia for Penelope. In all that time, before our last night together in Santa Fe, in all that time, I had never once made love."

Penny snorted. "You, a virgin for 3,500 years?! Please."

"Oh, Sappho," he chuckled, "Penny misunderstands. I had lots of sex. Several bedposts whittled to the ground. But she is the only woman with whom I have ever made love."

"Oh my God!" she exclaimed. "The same for me. I'd fucked before, of course, but never made love. That distinction — it's how I figured out I was in love with you."

"That's the difference between Penny and me, Sappho. I just knew I loved her. She had to reason it out. Not that I would want her any other way."

"Why are you talking to the dog?" she asked, annoyed.

Michael ignored her question, continuing to address Sappho. "We were reading the *Oresteia* by Aeschylus, discussing the trial in the last play. The jury is tied, and Athena, not of woman born, sides with Apollo, acquitting Orestes of matricide, and forcing the avenging Furies, the spirits of all that is uniquely feminine, deep underground. I watched Penny's mind at work as she realized that the play was intended to justify the Athenian patriarchy. Until then, Penny had identified with Athena, and she felt utterly betrayed. All this I witnessed, but there was more. I saw her marshaling her courage, accepting the reality that she would have to face the world alone, without the support of any god. That's when I knew, Sappho, that's when I knew I loved her."

Sappho squirmed and whimpered, turned her head and licked Penny's face, pleading for release, wanting no longer any role in keeping them apart. "It's ok, girl," Penny said, relenting. "you can go." And go she did, struggling free of the covering sheet and scampering down the bed, dropping to the floor and settling there.

"For the record," Michael said, "Aeschylus was a misogynist pig who slandered Athena as well as Apollo. I make a point at least once a year of visiting Sicily and spitting on his grave. If you like, I could introduce you to the real Athena. We could even ask her to officiate."

He kissed her then, and they made love. Not with the fervor and intensity of their first night together, which Penny now likened to

Beethoven's *Eroica*. This was more in the style of a Japanese haiku —
simple, elegant, and yet truly profound, enacting a promise of undying
love. Afterward, Michael propped himself on his elbows above her,
gazed longingly into her eyes and sighed. He told her that he'd been
wrong when he said there was no need to ask her to marry him. He
needed to ask, and he needed to hear her answer. "Penelope, will you
marry me?" The words plain and simple, but the absolute sincerity and
the complete vulnerability writ large on his face as he spoke, a vision to
behold. Watching the tears forming in his eyes, it was all she could do
to hold back her own. Finally, smiling shyly, she said, "Ok." Things
between them might have easily escalated then if not for Sappho, who,
sensing the celebratory mood, leapt back onto the bed and pounced
excitedly on the pair of them. After much laughing, crying, and
slobbering, they settled into a tranquil sleep, a horizontal stack of
spoons: man, woman, dog.

CHAPTER 5

T he sound of the shower greeted Penny, followed by the playful barking of Sappho in the backyard. Michael getting clean, Sappho chasing squirrels — all was right with the world, she thought, still drowsy with sleep. She recalled their lovemaking and Michael's sweet proposal, smiling to herself. That's when it hit her — what would she tell her parents? Michael emerged from the shower just then, not bothering with the boxers, momentarily distracting Penny from her panic, her eyes wide and feasting. But he had seen the look of horror on her face. "What's wrong?" he asked.

"My parents," she blurted out. "What can I say to my parents?"

Michael laughed, relieved.

"It's not funny!"

"You're right. I'm sorry." He paused to slip on his robe. Penny in bed and yelling at him was distracting. He wanted to tell her how sexy she looked, chastising him but thought better of it. Instead, he appealed to her reason. "Consider the facts. Your parents love you, more than Alice, if that's possible. Speak to them in the spirit of truth, a version that they can believe, what we have told your aunt. There will come a time when we can reveal the whole to all of them. But not yet."

He sat on the edge of the bed, took her hand. "We have known each other for four years. My job brought me to Santa Fe on a regular basis, perhaps to work at the lab in Los Alamos, if they press for that detail. Things only recently became intimate between us. Tell them of the child, now, or later — the fact is, Penelope, I would have asked you to marry me regardless of the child or the prophecy. If you like, tell them that I followed you to Boston to ask for your hand, without knowledge of the pregnancy. The point is, we are deeply in love. Trust me, they will want to see their daughter get married, if at all possible. And they will love the prospect of a grandchild. So ask them if they can spare a week sometime in the next month for an all-expense-paid trip to the Greek Islands to attend your wedding."

He leaned in and kissed her. "Let's invite Alice and Marisol and Sappho first — they may have some advice for approaching your parents. Now, it's time to get out of bed, unless of course you want to invite me back in." He grinned, she grinned, and it became clear that breakfast would have to wait.

ΩΩΩ

Flying first class definitely had its advantages. Penny was able to sleep comfortably for most of the Air France flight from Boston to Athens, and she had really needed the rest. Artemis had arranged the upgrade and was now offering her orange juice and a croissant. "Can I get you anything else?" she asked.

"How about a few days of peace and quiet."

Artemis chuckled. "I believe the gentleman next to you has programmed that into the plan, although based on prior experience, I suspect he will keep you rather busy at night." They both looked to Michael for his reaction, but he was dead to the world. In a quieter voice, she added, "You know, he watched you sleeping most of the night. Just sat there and watched, like a love-sick puppy. I would never have thought my brother would fall so hard for a strawberry blonde." Artemis smirked, Penny scowled, but both understood the gentle tease, an understated acknowledgment of their impending sisterhood.

THE OAR OF ODYSSEUS

Penny was looking forward to some serious beach time. She needed to decompress, to reflect on all that had happened, and all that lay ahead. She wasn't exactly worried, at least not in any specifically identifiable way. Despite the potential threat to her and those she loved, she felt safe with Michael and confident in the skill and commitment of the Amazons. In fact, she was brimming with confidence, which made her a little uneasy. A body memory. Barreling down Aspen Mountain, knowing every turn, every bump, poised to deal with anything unexpected, trusting her instincts — that's when it happened, the crash that had ended her Olympic dream. The loss of that dream had hurt her, more deeply than the injuries, but through conversations with her aunt the following summer, she had come to embrace it as an opportunity to broaden her vision, to open up new possibilities. She began then to rely more on her intellect, to develop it, and to trust it. Not as if she had lost confidence in her instincts exactly, more like a change in style, in the way she approached problems, as a way of maintaining control. She needed time to process the events of the last few weeks, the circumstances of which had required her to make quick decisions, as if she were back on that downhill course.

Having understood this, Michael had arranged for her to have most of a week of unstructured time to think. With the able assistance of Hermes, travel agent to the gods, he had taken complete charge of the wedding plans — indeed, all of their plans for the next month. Her parents, as well as Alice, Marisol, and Sappho, would arrive seven days hence, the wedding to follow in another four. Her family and friends would depart the following afternoon, then she and Michael would spend the next couple of weeks honeymooning in Greece and Italy. Hermes had taken care of all the necessary arrangements, including the plan to sneak Sappho aboard the plane; he would actually be flying the chartered executive jet from Ruidoso to Boston and on to Karpathos, Saria's sister island, and back again, under the alias, Herman Kogen.

Michael stirred at the squawking announcement of their final descent to Athens. Penny leaned over, tenderly kissing his cheek. "Thank you," she said.

Bleary-eyed and still half asleep, Michael asked, "For what?"

She had been thinking of all he had taken on in the last few days, and his thoughtful consideration of her needs, but his question raised a host of other more profound possibilities — his love, his love-making, the child she carried... the list was endless. She giggled. "This whole adventure started with my wish to thank you, so I better be careful what I say here."

"You're safe with me." He smiled.

"I suppose in some respects. At least until I kiss you. Isn't that what you told me?"

He laughed. "True enough. But no court would hold me responsible for my actions. Temporary insanity. Crazy for you."

Penny marveled at how incredibly sweet Michael could be. He was still the same man she had known as Professor Ambros: bold in his thinking, assertive, indomitable, determined. But all that was tempered now by a gentle tenderness and an absolute openness to her. Nothing withheld. She had demanded that of him, and by implication, of herself. It was the bedrock of their relationship, she realized, the ground upon which she had metaphorically stood when she consented to be his wife. "Artemis said you watched me sleeping."

"I did, for hours."

"Why?" she asked, genuinely curious.

Michael furrowed his brow, thoughtful. "That's kind of difficult to say. Why does one stand transfixed, watching a beautiful sunset, perhaps until nothing remains but darkness? Wonder?" He paused. "I suppose I watched you full of wonder. At the turn of events that brought us together. At my incredible luck at finding you after three millennia. At my boundless happiness at having done so." He reached over, gently rubbing his knuckles down her cheek, then placing his hand on her stomach. "And wonder at what we've created."

"You know, motherhood was never on my radar. I worry about what kind of mother I'll be."

"You will be a terrific mother." He took her hand and gazed with love and sincerity into her jade-colored eyes that brightened to emerald flecked with gold as the plane dropped through the cloud cover over Athens. "Aside from the fact that you are... well, you... you've had two superb role models — your mother and your aunt — and you will have more help than you can use, from your family and mine, and from the Amazons. You understand that our daughter will want for nothing of a material nature. You will love her, we both will, unreservedly. That is what she will need from us. In the end, she will find her own path because you and I, by our love and our example, will give her the tools to do that."

ΩΩΩ

The Air Aegean connection to Karpathos was quick and uneventful, excepting Penny's growing sense of excitement and anticipation. She'd never been to Europe or anywhere outside North America, and the customs lines in the Athens airport didn't really count. She'd caught a glimpse of Saria from the air, volcanic mountains and secluded beaches, seemingly uninhabited, and a better view of the whitewashed villages climbing the hills of Karpathos. But Penny finally felt she was setting foot on European soil as she and Michael exited the terminal, their luggage in tow. Having Googled images of Karpathos, she had expected ocean vistas and white sand beaches. What she saw was a parking lot. Michael placed a hand on her shoulder, a gentle restraint, and pointed her to the left. There, maybe 20 feet away, was a petite African woman with piercing dark eyes, softened by a warm smile, leaning against a Land Rover, a large black and white sheepdog sitting at her side.

"Who's that?" she asked, looking at what could easily be an ad for a safari adventure: the model with the long face and flawless mocha skin, narrow nose, cheekbones to die for, and windblown shoulder-length black hair, wispy and straight.

"Our ride. Wait here. First, we meet the dog, Selene. She's a Greek Shepherd, very protective of the herd. She knows me and will accept you once she gets your scent." As the dog padded slowly toward them, Michael whispered in her ear, "Lucky dog." He smirked, and Penny blushed. Selene nosed about, as dogs will, as the African beauty approached them, extending her hand. "You must be Penelope. I'm Athena." They shook, Penny speechless, her eyes widening. "Not exactly what you expected, am I?" Athena smiled.

"Um... I guess I thought you'd be... taller."

Athena laughed. A hearty, side-splitting laugh. "Polly told me you had a dry wit."

"Polly?" Penny giggled, looking at Michael, who actually blushed before turning to Athena with a stern look. "It's Michael, now," he said.

But Penny wasn't ready to let it go. "Polly?" she repeated.

"A pet name, for Apollo," said Michael, turning again to Athena, "which shall never be spoken again."

Athena smiled, and Penny giggled, and both said together, "Don't be so sure."

The narrow road from the airport to the town of Karpathos paralleled the coast for a short distance before rising up, weaving its way around and between low hills and valleys before climbing sharply, affording Penny a stunning panorama of the southeastern shoreline, the calm Mediterranean waters sparkling the full range of colors from turquoise to the deepest blue. And to the north, her first view of the white and clay-colored buildings of Karpathos, and the sheltered harbor there, where a fishing boat awaited to ferry them the 30 miles or so up the coast to Saria. According to Athena, the two islands used to be one, until an earthquake broke them apart — an event sometimes ridiculously attributed to her uncle, Poseidon. "You cannot trust anything the poets say about us. You think I burst fully grown from my father's forehead? What was Hesiod thinking?" Athena shook her head in mock disgust, eyes never leaving the twisting roadway, clearly focused on the precious cargo she carried, none but her immortal. "Plato was right. All poets are liars. Inspired, perhaps, but just as likely pandering to the masses."

"You do know that the man I fell in love with was a classics professor, and I his student."

Athena chuckled. "I'm aware. But what drew you together was something much stronger than a shared interest in the classics. Still, I would never question the value of that literature. Sophocles, Euripides, Sappho, Virgil, Ovid — they have important things to say. And I love Homer, perhaps the greatest storyteller of all time. But whatever truths their works reveal are not historical. The mythology they collectively created and drew upon cannot be relied upon as fact — far from it, in many cases, including mine. Your Michael told me Aeschylus ruined me for you."

"Your Polly seems to have told you a great deal about me," Penny said, turning to see if Michael was attending to their conversation. He was not. Given the racket of the engine, the rattle of the chassis, and the blustery crosswind, it was a wonder that she and Athena could hear each other. Besides, Selene had laid her head in Michael's lap, happily commanding his undivided attention. Penny smiled sweetly at the scene and returned her attention to Athena, who seemed to be engaged in an internal debate.

"He and I go way back," she said, finally, accompanied by a rueful smile. "We have very few secrets. And he's right... I better get used to calling him Michael." She paused, a deep breath, a decision made. "I was in love with him, you know."

"What?" said Penny, sharper perhaps than she intended, a consequence of surprise more than anger or anxiety.

Athena smiled. "Not to worry. It was a long time ago and very one-sided."

Was she worried? She was sitting next to the most beautiful woman she had ever seen, who also happened to be the Goddess of Wisdom, and who had just told her that she was once in love with her soon-to-be husband. Maybe a little. "Did you ever... um...?" she asked.

This time Athena laughed. "No! But not for lack of trying on my part. Nothing in my bag of tricks could get him into bed. It just took one kiss from you, I understand." She smirked.

"I think I will have to have a little chat with Michael about the sanctity of our bedroom," an annoyed Penny replied.

"Please, don't be upset. There were no details. He was telling me your love story — and, honestly, it brought tears to my eyes. I am truly happy for the two of you." As well as a little envious, she realized, as she waited a beat or two for Penny to calm down. "And you'll want to hear the rest of my unrequited love story. Michael, Apollo then, would not sleep with me for fear of ruining our friendship. He had feelings for me, just not the ones I wanted. Before he met you, sex for him was strictly recreational, without attachment — a pleasant diversion, like playing golf might be for a man today. A chance to encounter nature, get a little exercise, enjoy the views, and have a drink or two after the final hole." Athena gasped as she heard what she had said, quickly adding, "No crude pun intended." But then she chuckled as Penny giggled. "Really!" she insisted, but it was too late — they were both laughing.

ΩΩΩ

All Penny could do was to feast her eyes on the views from the fishing boat traveling up the coast. The beaches she expected from her visits to Google, but those photos did not do justice to the stark landscapes rising up behind them, or the quaint fishing villages nestled around hidden coves, or the larger towns in the distant hills, stacked white cubes, like so many Legos, set against dark jutting peaks. She tried to imagine what life was like there, in the villages and towns, so removed from her own experiences in New Mexico and Boston. She was sitting on the starboard side, on a bench of sorts, her hand in Michael's, Selene resting at their feet. Turning toward him, she asked, "What's it like, living here?"

"Away from the tourist centers, much like it's been for hundreds of years," he said, a little wistfully. "There is an immediacy to life on an island, and a fatalism. The simple pleasures of family, the taste of a newly ripened grape, the sight of a whale rising in the early dawn — such things are deeply felt, savored. As if to store up resilience to endure the inevitable tragedies wrought by Fate. Think of Marisol: she has lived what I am attempting to describe."

Actually, she had been thinking a lot about Marisol. How close they had become in such a short time, like sisters almost. Very intelligent, very kind, and extremely observant — nothing escapes her. And she exudes a kind of regal humility, ennobling the mundane tasks of maintaining a home. Alice and Marisol are like partners, she thought, each with their own duties, all of equal importance. Penny wondered how much of that deep mutual respect was rooted in their experiences of exclusion.

And then she considered Michael's words, immediacy and resilience, characteristics of children. Needless to say, children and their characteristics had also become topics of great interest. In any event, Marisol was childlike in some ways, and perhaps self-consciously so — "we all need to remember what it feels like to be a child," Penny recalled her saying. But those qualities in her have been tempered or transformed, perhaps by what Michael called fatalism. Children experience their world in the moment; they have not yet eaten from the apple of self-awareness, they cannot anticipate the worst that Fate might have in store for them. The resilience of childhood, coupled with the loving support of her aunt, had allowed Penny to recover from the loss of her Olympic dream. But to accept the total devastation visited upon her life by Hurricane Maria, and to move on with an openness to new opportunities, demanded of Marisol more than simply resilience. She was, and is, courageous in a rare and remarkable way. Resilience may be the root of courage, but courage must also require self-knowledge and, ultimately, the awareness of one's mortality.

That thought, and the anxiety accompanying it, stopped her. What, then, was she to make of the immortals? Are they incapable of courage? Or could the courage of immortals be of a different order? Or was she wrong about courage altogether? She had to calm down and uncover the source of her sudden panic. Michael had turned toward her with a questioning look as she took a couple of very deep breaths. Of course, she was thinking about Michael's choice — she still wondered about his sacrifice of immortality. Was it an act of courage? Framing the question and the deliberate breaths were enough to calm her, and she smiled and squeezed his hand reassuringly. Michael understood that she was thinking hard about something, struggling with something, but satisfied that she was no longer in danger of hyperventilating, he pulled her closer and let her continue, uninterrupted.

She would never forget that moment when she had asked about his choice. "Smart man, Odysseus," he had said, and she'd burst into tears, and she could feel her eyes tearing now. He would die for her, for the love of her. At the graduation ceremony, Michael had praised her courage to love and to be loved, words spoken to her parents that had the ring of truth at the time — at least that love took courage. Now she knew them to be true both in the abstract and in her own case. So, there was a reciprocal connection of some kind between love and courage. Her previous account had been wrong, or more likely, incomplete.

She needed to take a different approach. Courage is, by its nature, the overcoming of fear. Fear of death? Not always, for there are some things the loss of which is worse than death — at least according to the likes of Socrates. That was the mistake she made. Courage required self-knowledge, but not necessarily the knowledge of mortality. Courage is the overcoming of the fear of loss, generally. That works. At least it explains the relationship between courage and love. Love is a risky business, surrounded on all sides by the possibility of loss. What then is the attraction of love, she wondered, and immediately giggled, mumbling under her breath, but loud enough for Michael to hear, "Well, there is that."

"What?" he asked, puzzled.

"Fucking," she replied, smiling brightly.

Michael whispered salaciously in her ear, "You're thinking about fucking?"

"Don't get any ideas. Besides, we don't do that, remember?" She snickered. "Although, according to Athena, that was once a hobby of yours."

"A pastime, I suppose. A way of literally passing the time, a long 3,500 years until I met you."

He had told her this before, but it hit her now with new force. She was his first and only love. And so afraid of losing her, after 3,500 long years, he'd lacked the courage to tell her the whole story that Monday morning when he left. She'd already forgiven him that transgression, but now she understood better its cause — an intense and unfamiliar fear, the fear of losing his only love. She reached her hand behind his head, pulled him gently down into a soft kiss. "I'll always love you, you know."

Michael smiled. "I do. And I know you're working on something in that pretty head of yours, but we're almost there. Saria," he said, pointing forward over the bow as the boat made a 90 degree turn to the northwest, entering a narrow channel that to Penny's eye could not have been wider than a football field.

Michael stood, pulling Penny up with him, and they made their way carefully to the raised bridge, with barely enough room for them to stand behind Athena and Tika, the Amazon pilot. "I hear you're telling my bride stories," Michael chided Athena.

"Artemis arrives tomorrow or the next day. Between the two of us, we'll have Penelope well briefed before the big day," she teased in return.

The banter between old friends had a warm familiarity for Penny until she remembered just how old these friends were, and that they were both authors, in some meaningful sense, of Western civilization. Not to mention the fact that she was about to be married to one of them, the former God of Light and Prophesy. Here she was, on a fishing boat in the far reaches of the Mediterranean, chugging toward the last refuge of the tribe of Amazons, whose future queen she carried in her womb. None of which she would have believed possible if told a few short months ago. For a moment, she longed for a barstool at Harry's, but only for a moment. She'd had the courage to embrace her destiny, like Marisol, and this Olympic dream would not end on a mountain in Colorado, because this time she would not be alone.

Tika cut the engines as they neared the beach, letting the little fishing boat coast slowly toward the sand. Three Amazons patiently awaited them, one of whom Penny recognized as Dr. Zoya. Athena nodded to Selene, who leaped overboard into the gentle surf, bounding and splashing her way to shore and spraying the indulgent contingent there with a few furious doggy shakes.

"This is her home," Athena explained to Penny. "I had her on loan; she discourages unwanted attention."

Penny giggled, knowing exactly what she meant. "I know an Amazon barista who's quite skilled at discouraging unwanted attention."

"I heard about that." The two women exchanged meaningful looks as the boat grounded itself on the sandy bottom, the bow pushing its way onto the beach, just above the receding waterline. Athena immediately slipped from the bridge to the bow and jumped down to the sand, while Tika gathered the luggage, tossing each piece to Athena, who in turn loaded it in a wagon-like cart attached to a small electric ATV. Meanwhile, Michael led Penny back to the small latched gate near the stern on the starboard side, swinging it out, and stepping down into the shallow water. He reached up for Penny, surprising her by pulling her into his arms, cradling her as if to carry her over the first threshold of their new life together.

"I can walk," she said, laughing and encircling his neck with her arms. "You wouldn't want to get your shoes wet."

"Yours are."

"I'm used to it," he replied, wading through the shallow water to the dry sand, where the three smiling Amazons awaited.

"I understand that we are to entertain the mother-to-be of our queen, the beautiful Penelope, but who may I ask is the interloper bringing her forth?" This from the apparent leader of the group, a beauty herself, with the characteristic symmetrical oval face of the Amazons, but with a darker complexion, revealing a hairline scar running down her cheek. And unlike the dark curls of her sisters, she had long straight hair, jet black, matched by the color of her penetrating eyes.

"That would be me, Themis, now Michael Kalomoira, still brother of Artemis and son of Poseidon," he said, as he gently dropped Penny to her feet next to him. "And this is Penelope, the love of my now mortal life," he added proudly. "Penny, let me introduce Themis, Regent of the Amazons, and our hostess."

"I am honored," said Themis, deferentially bowing her head and extending her hand.

Penny, unused to such treatment and not knowing what to say, blushed, and taking Themis's hand, spoke from her heart. "It is my pleasure to be welcomed here." The handshake completed, Penny continued. "Before I knew of Amazons, other than in the pages of mythology, I sometimes imagined myself to be one, a woman warrior. However long it takes, I would hope that you and your sisters will instruct me in your ways so that I might someday be worthy of that title."

Michael stood frozen, beaming with pride, awed by the poise, sincerity, and simple elegance of his bride. Themis too was clearly impressed. "I have been told, by Athena herself, that you and she are much alike," she said. "I can well understand that now. On behalf of the Amazons, I welcome you to our home and would be greatly pleased to one day welcome you to our ranks." Then she added confidentially, "Just between us here, I suspect that will be sooner rather than later."

"What's this?" asked Athena, wading in among them, playfully. "What plot is this?"

Themis laughed. "No plot yet. We haven't even finished with introductions. Penelope, this is my assistant, Calliope, who will be motoring your luggage up the hill." Calliope and Penny exchanged pleasantries, and with a nod from Themis, Calliope headed for the ATV.

"And I believe you know Dr. Zoya," Themis concluded.

"Of course." Penny smiled.

"Helena, please. I came to look after you. I hope you don't mind. We are, as you now know, rather isolated, and while there are excellent medical facilities here, the doctors have no experience with obstetrics." A wry smile.

"I'm delighted to see you. And my father will be even more delighted; he's the worrier in the family."

After a few polite chuckles, they began the hike up the hill, Athena and Michael leading the way, with Helena in tow, and Themis and Penny together, rambling slowly behind. Selene was in herding mode, circling the small band, encouraging without much success the two laggers to keep pace. But Themis was taking the opportunity to describe the organization of life on Saria, and she was in no hurry.

"You and your guests will be staying in the Royal Pod, one of six residential pods. Each of these pods has a hexagonal courtyard, with single-story apartments built on each of the six sides. The apartments in the Royal Pod have one or two queen beds, a full bath, and a small kitchen. The apartments in the other pods can each accommodate four on bunk beds, but right now, there are no more than two to a room. These dormitory-style rooms have private baths with a shower and no kitchen. The six residential pods are sited on ancient terraces, at different levels, that circle a central pod, the heart of our main campus. Again, a hexagonal courtyard, bigger and covered, where we eat our common meals. And built on the sides, the main kitchen, the pantry, our medical facilities, laundry, and administrative offices. Everything has been designed with the principles of self-sufficiency and sustainability in mind. Composting toilets, gray water systems, rainwater collection — all of which support the citrus orchards you can see ahead of us now. Lemons and mandarins, mostly. The main campus has its own solar electric system, with panels on all the rooftops, and backup from our geothermal power plant, engineered by Hephaestus, Athena's brother."

"Athena has a brother?" a surprised Penny asked, as Selene nipped playfully at her heels.

Themis smiled. "Yes, contrary to the prevailing mythology. Zeus is their father, and Nekhbet, an Egyptian goddess, their mother. In fact, Athena, Hephaestus, Artemis, and Apollo, now Michael, grew up together. Poseidon fathered the twins with Leto, who disappeared more or less after they were born. Nekhbet took the four of them to Alexandria as infants and raised them to young adulthood there. They are very close — all of them."

"I had no idea."

"There is much for you to learn about us all and what we've built here over two decades. But perhaps that is enough for today. As you see, the others are waiting for us, somewhat impatiently, and it would be well for you to get settled."

CHAPTER 6

Penny awoke just before the sun cleared the horizon, gray dawn, her second night on Saria coming to a close. She had slept late her first night — 11 hours of uninterrupted sleep, after a huge fish dinner in the central courtyard with the 25 or so Amazons currently in residence and the three Olympians: Athena, Hephaestus, and Michael. According to Athena, the entire pantheon of Mt. Olympus still considered Michael one of their own, save the possible exception of Aphrodite. And, according to Dr. Zoya, Penny should consume fish no more than twice a week while pregnant, given the mercury contamination present to some small degree in all the world's ocean fish.

Odd that those two details would be the first things she remembered about that dinner, as she quietly made her way to the bathroom so as not to disturb Michael. In fact, she had talked with Helena Zoya about food, but only briefly about its relationship to her condition. Helena had encouraged her to listen to her body and to eat what it told her — except for too much fish, of course. And she had stocked the kitchen in their room with lots of breakfast foods, protein-rich snacks, and fresh fruit.

Much more interesting was what Helena knew about the system in place for feeding the Island's residents. The Amazons had a modest fishing fleet of three small boats, docked on the east side of the Island, their typical daily catch more than capable of supplying Saria's needs, the surplus delivered to the Amazon owned and operated resort on the big island, Karpathos. That resort was also home to a herd of goats, from which the Amazons made various cheeses and Greek yogurt. Finally, the Amazons harvested vegetables from their courtyard gardens and citrus from the surrounding orchards. Altogether, they produced roughly 80 percent of their nutritional needs.

She'd had an even more fascinating conversation with Hephaestus, who everyone called Harry, due no doubt to the fact that he was hairy, everywhere. A jumbled halo of twisting tufts of black hair, a wild afro, surrounded his square face, which sported a three-day beard. And curly black hair sprouted from his legs, arms, and chest where they were not covered by his khaki shorts and denim work shirt with rolled-up sleeves. He was solidly built, compact, not more than six feet tall, with the same mocha skin as his sister, but weathered and, well, hairy. Unlike his sister's sharp facial features, Harry's face projected a gentleness — a strong but dimpled chin, soft full lips, rounded nose, and sad eyes. At a distance, a bear of a man; close up, more like a teddy bear.

Harry had designed most of the systems on the Island, but was most proud of his geothermal electric plant. He had managed to tap into the heat of the magma pools under the Island to heat seawater, creating enough steam to power several large electricity-generating turbines. Nothing really unusual about that, he told her. But then he had fashioned a way to capture the steam and condense it, creating a supply of distilled water for use in all the bathrooms, and for laundry, dishwashers, and so forth. Saria was blessed with a small spring, which was reserved exclusively for drinking water; his distilled water was used for everything else. And the sea salt residue was wholesaled to distributors of gourmet spices. Power, water, and profit — an engineering trifecta, he proudly called it.

Sniffing the array of fragrant bath salts lining the narrow shelf next to the bathtub, Penny selected a lavender. She could not remember when she had last had a tub to soak in, and she was not going to let the opportunity pass another day. It was still cool enough to enjoy the warmth of the water, not to mention the tingling of the salts and the scent of summer lavender. Having risen at 10 the previous morning, she had opted to take a dip in the cove where they had landed, with a shower before the communal dinner. The hours between the swim and the shower, she had spent largely on her own, letting her mind wander, thinking about what she needed to consider, setting an agenda. The wedding ceremony and related matters topped her list, and today she and Athena would take that on together, in a shady spot overlooking the beach. Athena had promised to assemble a picnic lunch, to be overseen by the ever-vigilant Dr. Zoya.

As she relaxed in the tub, dawn finally breaking, Penny realized how much she liked Helena, in spite of herself. Her experience with doctors following her skiing accident had made her leery of physicians in general. Not that the injuries to her shattered knee and wrist were not competently repaired. The problem was that her knee and wrist were the patients, with no real attention paid to the needs of a 12-year-old girl with shattered dreams. Helena was not like that. The fact that as an Amazon she had a vested interest notwithstanding, Penny felt cared for, not just as a patient, but as a friend. All the Amazons treated her that way, with patience, openness, and kindness, as if she were already a member of their tribe. They were much like the guardians in Plato's *Republic*, she thought: kind and gentle with their friends, and ruthless in defense of them.

Just then, Michael pushed open the door and entered the steamy confines, sporting what he liked to call morning wood. Turning toward him, Penny gasped. "Whatcha got there?" she asked, smiling.

"A little something I thought you might like."

"I wouldn't call it little."

"Well, aren't you sweet," Michael smirked. "I could climb in with you," he suggested, hopefully.

"I don't think there's room for me, you and... that." She smiled. "Perhaps I could lend you a hand."

"Just a hand?"

Penny giggled, sliding up on her knees in the tub, her hands gripping the side facing Michael, and the confines got steamy in a whole new way.

ΩΩΩ

"It's beautiful!" Penny exclaimed. "Thanks for suggesting this."

Athena and Penny were standing in the shade of a small stand of ancient olive trees on the bluffs to the west of the cove. The thick gnarled trunks of the trees and their spreading branches were a treat enough to see, but the views were astonishing.

"Look there," said Athena, pointing to the southwest. "Do you see the unevenness on the horizon? The little bumps? That's Crete — maybe 70 miles away. There's an olive tree there said to be 4,000 years old. These are at least 700 years old, probably more like 1,000."

Closer to hand, across the narrow straights were the stark, desolate mountains of the northern peninsula of Karpathos, and closer still, the white sand beach below them, where a group of 12 Amazons were training. So skilled were they that deadly kicks and punches could be executed with speed and precision, yet held back at the last possible moment. Penny was transfixed. A part of her wanted to climb down and join in, but her duties lay elsewhere. She sighed and sat cross-legged on the blanket Athena had spread. "Michael wants to hold the ceremony on the beach," she said.

"You sound skeptical."

"Sun, sand," Penny said.

"What if there were a tent, a big tent, open on the sides, you know, like the Santa Fe Opera?" Athena said this with a sly smile.

Penny furrowed her brow, the reference to Santa Fe clearly a provocation. "What is it you really want to tell me?"

Athena did not hesitate. "Your freshman year, Michael's Western Civilization course, the young African-American girl sitting quietly in the back of the room — that was me."

"You were spying on me?" Penny snapped.

"I was observing you, at Michael's request."

Penny felt blindsided, yet again, and she was angry about that, at least she wanted to be. But Athena was apparently trying to put everything out on the table, to clear the air, as it were. That's why she had revealed her one-sided love affair with Michael, and now this. Penny understood and appreciated that and was curious, as always. "This was about the prophecy," she replied, finally.

"At first, but it quickly became about much more. Michael did not believe he could be objective about you as a student. Even after I left Santa Fe, he sent me your papers to assure himself that your work was as good as he thought." Athena paused, checking Penny's reaction, which she read as nonplussed. "Your work was that good, and more. I overheard what Themis said to you about me. I thought you would like to know on what my assessment was based."

"I hope you can imagine how weird this is for me."

Athena laughed. "I think I can; after all, our minds are quite alike. One more thing you should know. Michael had decided, soon after that day with Aeschylus, that he wanted to marry you, regardless of the prophecy. But he was not going to reveal his feelings to you until after you got your degree. He felt to do so would be unfair. All this he told me at the time. He had already planned the trip to Greece to tell the Council as much, after which he intended to follow you to Boston. Your toast and your kiss sort of short-circuited those plans. But things seemed to have worked out for both of you. I'm so glad, and a little envious, to be honest."

"Envious? Because I have Michael?"

"Because you have a partner with whom you can share... everything... without restraint. I think I would die for that, as Michael has chosen to do."

Penny took a moment to consider all that Athena had said. She had really learned nothing new about Michael; he had told her more or less the same account of the evolution of his feelings. And she knew Michael and Athena were close. But she now had an inkling of the extent of Athena's participation in his life, the part most relevant to Penny herself. "You're telling me all this, so I won't be surprised later on."

"Oh, I'm sure you'll be surprised," Athena chuckled. "After all, Michael has lived more than 3,500 years longer than you. I've told you things about my relationship with him that might trouble you so that you can begin to trust me, as someone who can offer you some perspective when you are surprised, and so that you're comfortable with me officiating at your ceremony."

Penny smiled. "Well, I think I've come to grips with the fact that I won't be the prettiest woman at my own wedding."

"Is that what you think? Tell me, what did you see when you first saw me in the airport parking lot?"

Penny giggled. "The perfect model for a safari adventure company ad."

"Exactly! You did not see the Goddess of Wisdom, a woman of great intelligence, with a wealth of knowledge and experience. Looking as I do is a distraction from who I am and a magnet for unwanted attention.

"When I look at you, your character is revealed to me. I believe that is true for anyone who pays attention, and trust me, your looks demand attention. A strong, confident woman looking out on the world with intelligent eyes, open and curious, and strikingly beautiful. The fire in your soul is everywhere apparent but softened by compassion, just as your hair does not flame but burns red nevertheless. And what shines brightest is your courage, the courage to show yourself, and the courage of a woman warrior, an Amazon."

Penny gasped, recalling that moment before the mirror in her Santa Fe casita, when she saw that in herself — saw herself as an Amazon, before any of this.

"No one can know for certain that the prophecy is true, not for many years," Athena continued. "Yet everyone here knows it's true, they see its truth in you. I am not seen for who I am; you are, and that is a rare and precious gift, the very essence of beauty."

Penny sat stunned. The Goddess of Wisdom, the genuine article, not the myth she had attached herself to for a time, the most beautiful woman in the world so far as she knew, had just told her, a simple mountain girl from Ruidoso, that she was a rare beauty — and this, just one among a slew of compliments. Her mouth was dry, she swallowed hard. "I'm... um... a bit overwhelmed," she managed to say.

"I'm not surprised," Athena said, smiling and reaching out to tenderly stroke her cheek. "You are the star. Everything that happens here in the immediate future will be about you. Enjoy it. And know that you are not alone. You have Michael, of course. Helena to look after your health, and all the Amazons, for that matter. And I hope you will consider me your friend and ally, my brother as well. That reminds me."

Athena reached into her backpack, pulled out a small box, and handed it to Penny.

"Oh, my God! They're beautiful!" Penny was looking at a pair of thin rose gold wedding bands, one wider than the other, but clearly matched. An inquiring look at Athena.

"Hephaestus made them for you. They're almost weightless, but the copper in the gold makes them quite sturdy. And they're engraved on the inside."

"He mentioned the possibility..." said Penny, still awestruck, examining the rings. The engravings were in Greek, she figured, two words: καλοσ χαλεπον.

"My brother is impulsive. Besides, he was quite taken with you at dinner the other night. He told me you asked sharp, intelligent questions. He's not used to that, except from me." She smiled.

"This is Greek?" asked Penny.

"Ancient Greek — an old saying. In English, it would sound like *kalos kalepon*. It means fine things are difficult — fine as in noble or worthwhile. Good things are worth the struggle." She shrugged.

"Like love," said Penny.

"Like many things," Athena added, thoughtfully. "Giving birth, loyalty, honor, justice, wisdom, a war to save the liberal arts."

"The good life, the moral life," Penny said, nodding.

"Exactly." Athena watched Penny fondling the rings, trying hers on, all with a girlish grin on her face. "If you don't like them, I can throw them in the ocean." She smirked.

Penny scowled playfully. "You will do no such thing. I'll have to think of some way to thank your brother." She giggled, recalling the last time she thought about a special gift.

"Sit by him again at dinner — that will do it. By the way, Michael would like Hephaestus to stand with him, like a best man, but only if you have someone in mind as a counterpart, a best woman, or maid of honor. Have you given that any thought?"

"I have. I was thinking of Marisol, but there's a problem.

"Oh?"

"Marisol is very smart and very observant. She spotted the Amazons watching us."

"Really! Impressive."

"Anyway, she'll know right away that there's more going on here than we've said, and I can't in good conscience ask her, if she believes that I don't trust her."

"Do you trust her?"

"Absolutely."

"Then tell her, and have some smelling salts handy." Athena smiled.

Penny laughed. "Actually, I'm thinking of telling my parents and Alice too. They're *mi familia*. They have a right to know."

Athena took a few moments to think things through. "Talk to Michael. He will no doubt tell you what I'm about to, that you have to do what you think is right. But he may have some suggestions as to how to make it sound credible.... You're hungry."

"I'm always hungry." Penny sighed. "But how did you know?"

"Because you're always hungry?" Athena laughed. "But also because you've been staring rather intensely at the picnic basket. Let's eat. We can discuss wedding plans over lunch."

Penny and Athena were of one mind about the ceremony as well as the sandwiches Helena Zoya had packed. The latter disappeared quickly. As to the former, they both were focused on bringing the two families together. Penny and Michael were already married, in all essential respects — they didn't need a ceremony for that, except to acknowledge and celebrate the union. Penny expressed her need to include her parents, her aunt, and Marisol in her future life with Michael, and in the life of their daughter. That would be possible in a meaningful way only if all of them could be incorporated into the fabric of Mt. Olympus and Saria, recruited for the war, as it were. And that presupposed that she tell them all the whole truth. That much seemed settled.

They both offered specific details and suggestions and together crafted the outlines of a ceremony. The more they talked, the more Penny appreciated just how much they did think alike, and how much she valued Athena's insight. Well, she thought, they don't call her the Goddess of Wisdom for nothing. Athena agreed to take on the organizational tasks, assigning Penny the job of relaxing and looking after herself — a chore she readily accepted, at least in the short term. They had just finished up when they saw the fishing boat carrying Artemis heading for the cove.

ΩΩΩ

Dinner that night was in honor of Artemis, whom the Amazons all clearly adored. *Gyros* and *dolmas*, her favorite foods, were on the menu, and she had the seat of highest honor, where Penny herself had sat that first evening. She was in full flower, enjoying the attention and the accolades, regaling the multitude with flight attendant tales amassed over 20 years. And looking so young, but still very much like Tina Fey.

On the walk up from the cove, Artemis had explained to Penny that she was now officially retired from Air France, and therefore had no more need to disguise her age. "You don't look a day over 3,534, that's for sure — like Tina Fey when she was younger," Penny had said, playfully. To which her soon to be sister-in-law had replied: "Tina Fey is Greek, you know, on her mother's side, and it's Tina Fey who looks like me."

Athena had gone ahead to alert the troops that their general was on the way — her words. She'd given Penny instructions to walk slowly and keep Artemis talking, which would be an easy task, as Penny knew her companion would adhere to her pace, and Artemis loved to talk. Besides, she had interesting things to report, and Penny wanted to hear it all.

Turned out that Artemis was returning with them to Boston to take personal charge of the security operation there. She was looking forward to spending some quality time with Penny and Michael and drinking quality coffee at Cynna's place. Best of all, Aphrodite seemed to have fallen for their elaborate decoy operation, and was even now heading to Montreal. To less inquiring eyes, she appeared to be tracking a lesbian couple, living quietly in a rented flat in a working-class neighborhood. The pair were in fact Amazons, with two more nearby, standing watch. The neighbors, if asked, would recall that Jennifer Smith arrived first, sometime in mid-May, newly pregnant. Her partner, Sara Hansen — tall, broad-shouldered, and very butch — showed up a couple weeks later and worked part-time in a nearby warehouse.

The real Jennifer Smith had been an assistant librarian at the College of St. Frances, and was not pregnant — although certain hard to obtain but reliably authentic medical records suggested otherwise. She flew to Boston, where she joined a group of Mormon missionaries, and was now somewhere in Africa. Amazon Jenny had secured a

Canadian passport in Boston, from one James O'Reilly, known to do contract work for Mt. Olympus Security, LLC, and had taken a bus from Boston to Montreal. Sara Hansen had no existence at all before also acquiring a Canadian passport from Jimmy O'Reilly, renting a car in that name, which she dropped off in Portland, Maine, where she boarded a bus for Montreal. Curiously, Sara's apparent emergence from thin air occurred shortly after Michael Kalomoira, traveling on an American passport from Athens, had arrived at Logan International Airport in Boston.

Shortly after preparing the two Canadian passports, James O'Reilly had been seduced by a young woman, who apparently shared his taste for Irish whiskey. They had gone back to his apartment, which was also his place of work, where he awoke the following morning alone and quite hungover — something special had been dropped into his last shot, no doubt. He supposed that his studio had been accessed, and his recent work for Mt. Olympus Security compromised, earning him a tidy cash bonus. Much had been done to cover the tracks of the two Amazon principals, to obscure the trail of breadcrumbs and render them difficult to follow — all to persuade the clever sleuth that was Aphrodite that she was in fact uncovering the truth. Disguising "Michael" as a butch lesbian was the pièce de résistance.

Artemis had not noticed the welcoming assembly, so immersed in the telling of her tale she was, but hearing the applause of the two lines of Amazons flanking the entrance to the main campus, fronted by Themis, with the three Olympians arrayed just behind her, she had looked up, both surprised and pleased, and cried out above the din: "Oh my! Thank you! It's so good to be home." After a brief pause, she had added, to roars of laughter, "And just think, Air France will be paying my pension forever!"

Now the evening's festivities were coming to a close. Penny cornered Hephaestus at the dessert table, where they both sliced off generous servings of cheesecake and settled at an empty table on the courtyard's fringe. "Artemis has certainly received a hero's welcome," Penny noted between bites.

"Well deserved," Harry replied. "She's spent the last 20 years traveling all over the world, providing encouragement and direction, giving them hope... and now, she's given them you."

Penny blushed. "Will she really be getting a pension?"

"Not forever," Harry chuckled. "She has 20 years in and the French are generous, and no one will question that she might live to a ripe old age. Maybe 50 years of payments, a substantial sum in the end."

"Where will the money go?"

"Directly into one of our Swiss bank accounts. We use Swiss banks for all of our legitimate businesses."

"Just how many businesses do you have?"

Harry smiled. "Well, the Karpathos resort and the sea salt concession, you know about, and Dr. Zoya's Fertility Institute, Cynna's coffee shop — together they generate a modest income. The Amazons' main source of operating funds is Mt. Olympus Security — Artemis's baby. There's some personal security work, which can be quite lucrative, but usually short term. Her main business is cyber security." Hephaestus raised an eyebrow, studied Penny's reaction. "Maybe your bold analytical mind can tell you who her main clients are."

Realization dawning, Penny replied, "Banks."

"Located?"

"Switzerland... and the Caribbean."

"Correct." He smiled. "Bermuda and the Cayman Islands, to be precise. And the last piece of the puzzle is the Bunker, which you have yet to see. Below ground, invisible from the air, impenetrable by any known electronic means, and with enough electrical power to run an impressive array of state-of-the-art servers and keep them cool. Moving money from one bank account to another is child's play. Covering the tracks, or even better, attributing the act to specific and deserving targets — that's a whole other thing. But that's exactly what we plan to do."

Penny sat stunned, a fork full of cheesecake suspended midway between the plate and her mouth. She now knew the whole game plan, but was only beginning to understand the depth of the planning, the forethought, and the patience that went into it. "But surely the income from what you've described could not have built... all this."

"Correct again. Your analytical skills are as advertised. We Olympians have considerable real estate holdings and a raft of tourist-related enterprises — resorts, travel and tour agencies, a charter air company, and so on. About eight percent of the annual revenue from those assets is skimmed and deposited in Cayman Island accounts held by the Amazons. That money is invisible to the authorities and has been sufficient to fund all the capital projects here. You can now see that, with the exception of Aphrodite, we have the full, if sometimes begrudging, support of the pantheon of Mt. Olympus."

Penny nodded, taking in the magnitude of the undertaking she, and soon her family, would be party to. She felt a little overwhelmed, which, truth be told, she was becoming much accustomed to of late.

"For the sake of completeness, there are a number of Amazons working independently, in sensitive diplomatic and political settings," Harry continued. "Their incomes are held individually, until they retire, like Artemis, or until they are otherwise separated from their positions.

Finally, as I think you know already, we fund the continuing education of between 10 and 20 Amazons at cutting-edge research universities throughout the world."

Penny looked at Hephaestus with something like awe, but certainly respect. And then she recalled why she had cornered him in the first place. Leaning toward him, she kissed him on the cheek. "Thank you for the rings. A beautiful gift from a beautiful man." She thought she saw him blush, but she could not be sure.

CHAPTER 7

P enny and Michael waited on the tarmac with the resort's minivan as the twin-engine Gulfstream taxied up to the private terminal. Hermes, aka Herman Kogen, flew in and out of Karpathos all the time and had an arrangement with the security and customs officials. That's why they were able to drive onto the tarmac after a brief check at the gate, and why they would be able to leave with their passengers in like manner. It was quite early, not yet 6 a.m. local time. They would have left Boston in the afternoon, and with the time change and the eight or so hours in the air, cheated the night. Penny hoped that everyone had been able to sleep, excepting the pilots, of course. A big day was ahead of them, bigger than any of them could probably imagine. It was to be the day of the big reveal.

The plan was for all of them to spend the day on Karpathos and stay the night at the Amazon owned resort, the Palace — actually in Greek, Παλάτι Αιγών, the Palace of the Goats. Penny wanted to get Marisol alone for a time, on the ferry or perhaps visiting the goats, to tell her first. Coming from the Caribbean, Michael thought Marisol would be familiar with notions of living spirits, magic, and fatalism, and therefore more open to the truth of Penny's tale. Later, after dinner, with Marisol by her side, Penny would tell her parents and her aunt.

The plane pulled to a stop, engines cut, and the stairway pushed against the hatch and locked into place. Penny and Michael walked in that direction as the door opened and Sappho came charging down the stairs, dragging her leash, apparently pulled suddenly from Alice's hand if the accompanying screech was to be believed. Sappho made short order of the distance between them, dancing and jumping around Penny and Michael as if they were doggie treats of the finest quality. Laughing, Penny knelt and embraced the squirming dog, as Michael fumbled for the leash, finally securing it, but with little effect on the dog's excitement.

"You wonderful sweet dog. You seem quite happy to see us. Or maybe just to be on solid ground," said Penny, looking up at Michael. "And she probably needs to pee."

"Good point. We'll make sure before we leave. Come, let's greet your parents."

Introductions were pro forma, for the most part. Siobhan, Penny's mother, embraced Michael warmly; her father, Frank, scrutinized him appropriately. They had counted on the long plane ride with Alice and Marisol, who had lived with them for several weeks, to vouch for Michael and the authenticity of their love. And to avoid too many embarrassing questions during the drive to the harbor at Karpathos, Penny planned to ride next to her father, with Siobhan up front with Michael. The one surprise was Cynna, who, along with managing the coffee shop on the BU campus, was a certified pilot and had signed on as copilot for the chance to visit her home and attend the wedding. She was hoping to hitch a ride to the Palace, where she had already arranged to bunk with Athena. Fortunately, the minivan had seats for seven and plenty of willing laps for Sappho. Luggage was offloaded, scanned, and secured on the roof rack, passports quickly reviewed at the security gate, and they were off to catch the auto ferry to Diafani, famous for its beach and home to the Palace.

The short trip to the harbor was relatively uneventful. Siobhan predictably asked about the wedding plans. Michael told her that Penny and his cousin, Athena, who would officiate, had things well in hand, but he knew nothing of the details. Penny kept her father occupied with questions about her friends back in Ruidoso. As he filled her in, she realized how far from that life she had come. At one point, she had despaired about not having any of her friends from home, or even her college friends from Santa Fe, at her wedding. But she realized that everyone who was truly important to her now would be there. Conversation all but died when the van started the steep climb that afforded the views of the coastline and the Mediterranean beyond.

Soon the van was safely parked on the lower deck of the Diafani ferry, and its occupants were making their way to the upper deck as the boat churned away from the dock.

Michael and Cynna took turns narrating the trip north for Alice and the Bauers, pointing out villages, geologic features, hidden coves, the secret nude beach everyone knew about, recounting history, ancient and modern, and describing contemporary demographic trends and economic conditions. Meanwhile, Penny managed to slip away with Marisol for a little quiet chat.

"I have some things I need to tell you," Penny said, after assuring that they were out of earshot.

"I am sure you do," said Marisol, to Penny's questioning look. "Cynna told me, by mischance I am sure, that she has roughly one hundred sisters."

Penny nodded, resolved. "Cynna is an Amazon — a real Amazon, as were the group you spotted in Cambridge, as are the 25 or so we will meet tomorrow on Saria, their last stronghold. Cynna is one of the youngest, approximately 3,000 years old. There is more to this story, much more, and I want to tell you everything. Once you know it all, I want to ask you to stand with me at my wedding, as my maid of honor. Perhaps later, after everyone is settled, we can visit the herd of goats belonging to the Palace, and talk then."

Marisol took Penny's hands in hers. "You will tell me what you need to; I shall keep an open mind. And I would be honored to stand with you in any event."

ΩΩΩ

The guests from America were escorted by Anaxilea, the Palace's manager, to the Royal Suite. There they found a fully-stocked wet bar and bowls of fresh fruit in the main sitting room, flanked by bedrooms on either side, each with its own bathroom, and a large balcony overlooking the beach. Michael had told them that everything was paid for, so they should enjoy themselves, especially as no alcohol was permitted on Saria. He didn't tell them that part of the reason for spending their first night here was the availability of strong drink to accompany the tale they would hear that evening.

After refreshing themselves and unpacking, they joined Penny and Michael for a lavish brunch of *meze* and *moussaka* — the former a huge platter of roasted vegetables, stuffed grape leaves, olives, feta, pita, and a number of dipping sauces, the latter an eggplant and potato casserole. Alice and the Bauers announced their intention to spend the afternoon at the beach, swimming and sunning, and otherwise just relaxing. Penny wanted to show Marisol the goats and the dairy facilities, and wanted Sappho to come with them. Michael needed to catch up on some work, so he would hole up in his and Penny's room with his laptop. They all agreed to meet for dinner and then for an update on the wedding plans in the Royal Suite.

ΩΩΩ

At first, Sappho did not know what to make of the goats. After all, she had never seen a goat before. But they didn't seem dangerous; in fact, they seemed to barely notice her, which truth be told was a little hurtful to her doggie pride. On the other hand, they were drawn to

Marisol, who greeted them warmly, with soft words and gentle pats to their heads and strokes to their long necks. Sappho could use a bit more of that. She whimpered.

Penny knelt, scratching her behind her ears, rubbing her all over. "Are you feeling left out? A little jealous?"

Exactly. Penny and Sappho were both Irish mutts and both redheads. Of course they understood each other. Marisol was friendly and sweet enough, but Sappho found her always to be a bit aloof.

Penny removed her leash. "You be a good dog now, stay close. Marisol and I are having an important conversation. Very important. Let us do this, and I'll ask Alice if you can sleep with Michael and me tonight."

Sappho communicated her delight. That was the other thing she had in common with Penny — they both loved Michael.

Penny was engaged in a serious conversation, but for the most part, one-sided: she was talking, Marisol listening, respectfully and thoughtfully. Penny had considered what she would say to her parents, a much-edited version of what she was saying now. Marisol was getting her personal story -- from her relationship with Professor Ambros and the night of unbridled passion, through her own struggles in accepting the truth of her situation, and even Marisol's own role in convincing her of the justice of the coming war. Marisol would be standing with her at the wedding and sitting with her this evening. Asking this of her, Penny realized, meant that she was now and would most likely remain forever, her closest and dearest friend; she deserved no less than the whole story. That story was coming to a close when Penny noticed Athena exiting the barn, with Selene at her side, casually walking in their direction.

"Looks like you'll get to meet Athena," Penny said to Marisol and knelt again to Sappho, embracing the now very alert dog in her arms. "And you, Sappho, you're going to meet Selene. She's a shepherd, bred and trained to guard the herd. You must approach her cautiously, but show your Irish character and do so fearlessly."

Looking up across the field, Penny caught Athena's eye; she had also knelt, addressing Selene. Both thinking the same thing, no doubt, they released their dogs, who padded slowly toward each other. The goats, at least most of them, sensing the import of the moment, turned their attention to the coming encounter. The dogs touched noses, like kissing Eskimos, then circled each other, finally sniffing butts, like... well, like dogs. Then, somewhat surprisingly, they sat side by side, but facing their respective mistresses, as if to say, "We're cool, so set us free to romp and play." Athena gave Selene a nod, as Penny said, "Ok, girl," and that's exactly what they did, racing around, nipping at each others' heels, and rolling around in the grassy stubble.

Athena laughed. "That's got to be a good omen," she said, joining the others.

"This is Marisol, who has agreed to stand with me," said Penny. "Marisol, meet Athena, the Goddess of Wisdom."

"I can see that," Marisol said, extending her hand after an assessing look.

Athena took her hand, tilted her head, and narrowed her eyes. "You're a seer."

"My grandmother and my mother were said to have such talent," Marisol replied.

Penny's eyes grew big and she swallowed hard as she watched the exchange between these two with wonder.

"And what is your take on what I assume you have just heard?" Athena asked.

"The truth spoken by Penelope is easy to accept."

Athena smiled, turning to Penny. "You choose your friends wisely." Then back to Marisol. "The others? How do you imagine they will hear it?"

Marisol took a moment to consider. "Alice will believe it, especially with the two of us together. I have only just met Penny's parents, but I suspect her mother will be enchanted, her father skeptical."

Penny laughed. "My father has a hard time believing I'm not still 12. But he is an engineer, rational to a fault. He will be convinced by the facts on the ground, if not by the withering stare of my aunt or my mother's gentle teasing."

"And what do you propose to tell them?" asked Athena gently.

"All the essential facts, including our plan to engage in cyber warfare, withholding only the specific strategy for now, unless pressed. I would like to speak to them with Marisol at my side but without your presence or Michael's. However, I would ask that you both come in when I am finished to answer any questions they might have."

Athena marveled at Penny's clarity of speech, knowing that she had prepared for this day, that she had thought things through at least a dozen times, that she was ready. "Then that is what we shall do," she said.

ΩΩΩ

"Where's Michael?" asked Alice when she opened the door of the Royal Suite to Penny, "and Athena? She's a hoot, that one."

"They will be along in a little while," replied Penny as she entered, giving her aunt a kiss on the cheek. "I was hoping to have a word with you all before then."

"Of course, sweetheart," said Siobhan, coming forward for her own kiss. "Shall we sit?"

Penny slipped in next to Marisol on the love seat directly opposite the leather sofa, where her mother and her aunt sat side by side, her father taking the matching armchair angling off to the right. "First, I want you to know that Marisol has agreed to stand with me as my maid of honor. She has also agreed to sit with me this evening because she has heard what I am about to tell you, and I think she believes it to be true."

"I do," Marisol said simply, taking Penny's hand in hers.

Penny took a deep breath before launching into her tale, using the opening she believed Athena had prepared for her. "The stories Athena told at dinner of growing up with Michael were true, but lacking in two important respects: she knew Michael as Apollo then, and the events took place over 3,000 years ago. In the prevailing Greek mythology, Athena is the Goddess of Wisdom, the genuine article. Her brother Hephaestus is the God of Fire, and Artemis, Michael's twin sister, the Huntress, is the Goddess of the Moon — both of whom you will meet tomorrow. The pilot Herman Kogen, who flew you here, is really Hermes, the Messenger and God of Travel. Michael used to be Apollo, the God of Light, but he gave up his powers and his immortality to be with me. In short, the 12 gods of the Olympian pantheon are still with us, 11 of whom are immortal and possessed of certain powers, probably much more limited than you might imagine. Athena and Michael can elaborate later and answer your questions. For now, I ask only that you accept this truth provisionally so that you can hear and understand the rest of my tale in the proper context."

She looked at the stunned faces, the wide eyes of her parents and her aunt, the silence broken only by the distant breaking of gentle waves upon the sandy beach. Because their reaction was what she expected, she felt herself relaxing, and she smiled. "If anyone needs a drink, now might be the time to get it." That at least elicited a chuckle from Alice, who retrieved the Irish whiskey and three glasses from the bar, pouring a healthy portion into each and handing one to her sister and one to Frank, then sipping her own.

Penny began again, first describing the Amazons, their organization and history, the fact that the Palace was one of several businesses supporting the tribe. She spoke about the values of the Olympians, their view of the good life, the moral life, referring in passing to what her parents might remember of that from the commencement address at her graduation, and about the Amazons' role in defending those values. Then she told them of the ancient prophecy. Siobhan gasped, a hand flying to cover her mouth, as realization dawned.

"My child may very well be the fulfillment of this prophecy, although we won't know for many years yet. And even if she proves to be immortal, no one will force her to accept the mantle of Queen of the Amazons, least of all the Amazons. To their family and friends, they are exceedingly kind and gentle and deferential. You will see this for yourselves tomorrow. And I am telling you all of this because Michael and I want you to be involved in our lives and the life of our child. She will know you, she will learn from you as I did, and she will find her own path, as you made it possible for me to do."

"The danger," interjected Alice, "it's really about your baby, isn't it?"

"Yes, *Tía*," Penny answered, pausing briefly to collect her thoughts. She told them of Aphrodite and her psychopathic impulse to derail the birth, for only after birth would the child be immortal. Accordingly, Amazons had been deployed to protect all of them in this room, as Alice and Marisol already knew. Penny added that an elaborate decoy scheme designed by Artemis seems to have drawn the attention of Aphrodite, which meant, if nothing else, that she had not yet discovered who carried the child. To lighten the mood, Penny recounted the episode with Cynna in the coffee shop and assured them all of the Amazons' competence and commitment.

"You may think that I have lost my mind, or have been seduced or brainwashed to join some fantastical cult, but a moment's reflection about who I am, who you raised, should convince you otherwise. You also need to understand that, barring the operations of Fate, I initiated the events that have brought me, and now you, to this point. Granted, I did not at the time know the full consequences of my actions, but I have come to embrace them with my whole heart, and I hope you will as well.

"One last piece. Twenty years ago, Michael and Artemis convinced the Olympian Council to revive interest in the ancient prophecy in an effort to mobilize and energize the Amazons in defense of the classical vision of the good life. You will see first-hand the fruits of their efforts tomorrow, all directed finally to a bloodless war, a cyber war aimed at promoting liberal arts education around the world — the liberal arts being the means to reinvigorate a commitment to the values of the Olympians. Mom and Dad, you may recall the mention of such a war at the conclusion of the commencement address at my graduation."

"Wait a minute," Frank blurted out. "That professor, your professor — wasn't his name Michael?"

Penny smiled and blushed. "Yes... and now you know it all."

There was a knock at the door, and Michael and Athena strolled in, not waiting to be invited. "We heard Frank shout," said Michael, casually, not displaying any real concern. "Thought we'd better find out what was happening in here."

Penny narrowed her eyes at him, but Frank just laughed. "So you're Penny's old Professor — old being the operative word there," Frank quipped, but with a bit of an edge.

"I was," replied Michael, "and your daughter will tell you our relationship was exactingly professional until after she got her degree."

"But you look much younger now," Frank said, curiosity replacing any hint of challenge.

"Oh, that." Michael smiled and proceeded to explain the powers of the Olympian gods that he no longer had. "I'm as mortal as you now, Frank, and aging every day."

"I don't understand where you come from." Siobhan's first words.

Michael looked to Athena, clearly deferring, and discreetly edged himself onto the arm of the love seat next to Penny. Still standing, as if at the head of a classroom, Athena took control of the room. "Well," she said, "Michael and I, and all the Olympians you will meet here, are second generation, so we know our parents. But I suspect that's not what you are asking. The origin of gods like us is a question without a clear answer. What I will say is this: all great civilizations have produced, or are produced by, a pantheon of immortals who hold and carry the values of that civilization. I speak of a kind of cultural immanence or dialectical necessity. We provide the institutional memory, as it were, the continuity between generations necessary for a civilization to flourish. And when the civilization declines and dies, its gods fade and disappear. My mother was the Egyptian goddess Nekhbet. She perished with that civilization. And that has been happening to the gods of the West for some time now, as the values of the good life as we understand it have been undermined and diminished, replaced by the values of money and status and power. We Olympians are the last, as far as we know, along with our loyal defenders, the Amazons.

"The gods I speak of are, of course, pagan, quite apart and different from the transcendent gods of the Old and New Testaments. We have no interest in theology, only in the ethical or moral life, what the philosophers of ancient Greece called the character virtues: honor, loyalty, courage, justice, self-control, and wisdom. Penelope displays all of these qualities in the way she leads her life; she is, as the prophecy proclaims, a woman of high character. Perhaps she believes in the Christian God, perhaps not. Either way, she is an exemplar of the good life, as we understand it. With the help of the Amazons, we hope to restore that vision of the good life to its proper place of eminence in the rubric of Western culture."

"And what does Fate have to do with all this?" asked Alice.

Athena smiled. "Three questions, one from each of you, and all knocking at the door of truth — no, not knocking, pounding. No wonder Penelope has grown to be the remarkable woman she is." Athena looked at Penny, who blushed, of course, as Michael took her hand, and then began again, having taken that moment to consider her reply.

"What causes an apple seed to grow into an apple tree? Water, nutrients from the soil, exposure to the sun — these conditions are necessary, but in the absence of the apple seed will not produce an apple tree. The seed contains the potential, in its nature or its character. And the seed is not passive. As it sprouts, it will literally seek out the water, the nutrients, the sun it needs. This seeking too is part of its nature or character. The fate of the apple seed is to become an apple tree, not an oak, not a larch. Will the apple seed become an apple tree? Conditions must be right, to be sure — but much will depend on the strength or character of the seed itself.

"With human beings, it is much the same. A person can be said to have a calling. Does everyone find their calling, their purpose in life? Of course not; conditions must be right. But much depends on the strength and character of the person.

"About 3,000 years ago, a priestess of Apollo proclaimed at Delphi the prophecy of which we are all aware. She would have known the character of my cousin, Apollo, the God of Light. She would have known his calling, to bring light to the world, and who he might seek to help him in that quest, and what sacrifices he would be prepared to make. She would have also known the tragedy that had befallen the Amazons, the death of their twin queens at Troy. She had an insight.

"The fact that we are all together in this room tonight, and in a few days will be celebrating the union of Penelope and Michael, who have discovered their shared calling, could be the consequence of a series of random events. Just as we might explain the presence of an apple tree in the middle of a conifer forest. Even so, I will assert, unequivocally, that much depended on the strength and character of these two individuals. And that is what I say to you is the meaning of Fate."

Sappho, who had been lying by the open doors to the balcony, stood and stretched, then padded softly through a room pregnant with quiet reflection, and laid down again at Athena's feet. The dog had spoken the last word, and everyone laughed.

ΩΩΩ

Tika met the entourage with her fishing boat mid-morning at the Diafani dock, for the hour-long journey to Saria. Athena had told Alice and the Bauers to ask questions of anyone and everyone on the Island, assuring them that they would hear frank and honest answers. Once on board, they wasted no time taking her advice, peppering Cynna with questions about her life as an Amazon. Alice seemed to be especially attentive. For her part, Cynna fielded the queries with grace and openness. Penny marveled at how such a gentle soul had so decisively taken down her would-be suitor at the coffee shop.

On the opposite bench, Michael feigned disquiet at Marisol's presence, having been determinedly shooed by her from the suite the previous evening, so that Penny could try on the wedding dress Alice and Marisol had made for her. Penny had been surprised to learn that Michael had left instructions that the dress should be appropriate for a beach ceremony, including a brief walk through the shallows. She playfully teased him about making such presumptions without consulting her, to which he replied that he just wanted to see her barefoot and pregnant on the beach, if not in the kitchen. But then he spoke more candidly of the importance to him of stepping from the water.

"You know Poseidon is my father; I am quite literally a child of the water. Even the stars say so. I'm a Scorpio, a water sign."

"I thought you didn't know your birth date."

"I don't, not exactly. My passport says October 29, which is an approximation. I was born under a different calendar than the one in use now." He smirked. "Artemis might know. We do have that date in common. You, my love, are an Aires, a fire sign, the better to boil my blood. And Mars is our ruling planet — yours and mine. According to the stars, the father of the Amazons rules our destiny, if you believe in that sort of thing."

Penny smiled. "I believe in you and me together." Sappho raised her head and boofed. "And Sappho, of course," she added. Mollified, Sappho snuggled up again against Selene in the bay between the benches, the two of them apparently enjoying the relaxing rhythm of the boat's gentle rocking.

But doggie nap time was short-lived, for Tika was turning into the narrow channel separating Saria from Karpathos, and activity on-board took on a new urgency. Athena stepped down from the bridge to review the protocol for the welcoming ceremony. The key points were that

Penny alone would introduce her family, and Themis would introduce her companions and offer welcome. Once that welcome was accepted, the formalities would be complete, and everyone could relax. Cynna, who was to stay aboard with the two leashed dogs until that point, could then set them loose.

As soon as the boat coasted into the beach, two Amazons wrapped thick ropes around the bow cleats and tied them to posts pounded deep into the sand on either side. Another two secured a railed plank ramp to the bow, and the passengers began to descend. Flanked by Athena and Michael, Penny led the group toward the welcoming committee of four, waiting patiently under the morning sun.

"Penelope," said Themis, "you have guests from America."

"I do," she responded. "My parents, Siobhan and Frank Bauer, my aunt, Alice O'Connor, and my friend and confidant, Marisol Rivera."

"I am Themis, Regent of the Amazons." A deferential nod. "To my right, is my assistant, Calliope, and to my left, Artemis, daughter of Poseidon and sister of Michael, and Hephaestus, son of Zeus and brother of Athena. Welcome to Saria, home of the Amazons. Please make any needs you might have known to Calliope or me, or to any of our sisters."

Siobhan stepped forward, extending her hand. "Thank you. We are honored to be here and welcomed by such a noble gathering. And we are most grateful for your hospitality."

Themis took her hand and replied, in a quiet voice, woman to woman, "We are grateful for your daughter."

Whatever remained of formality or tension was quickly dispelled by the antics of the two dogs, who leapt from the boat and raced in circles around the assemblage, kicking up sand, before exuberantly darting into the surf to play among the gently breaking waves.

"And who might be the red-haired beast cavorting with Selene?" asked Themis.

Penny laughed. "Her name is Sappho, a dog of uncommon wisdom and judgment, and of great service to Michael and me."

ΩΩΩ

After the new arrivals settled in, tours of the Island became the subject of discussion. Frank and Marisol were keen to join Hephaestus for a look at his geothermal operations. Penny thought she noticed Marisol smiled a little brighter, and her caramel-colored skin glowed a little warmer. Artemis offered to show the others around the main campus, which suited Siobhan and Alice. Athena had wedding plans to see to, and Penny, blushing slightly, suggested a nap for herself and Michael.

Frank, an engineer himself, was duly impressed by what Hephaestus had designed and built, asking insightful questions, which Harry answered as best he could, given the distraction of Marisol's presence and the looks she flashed him. There was definitely something about her, and when Frank was studying the multitude of gauges in the control room, Harry stole a moment alone with her. "You're a seer," he said.

Marisol laughed, her best flirty laugh. "Nothing gets past you Olympians, does it? Your sister said the same thing to me when we met."

"Because it's true. So, tell me, what do you see?"

"A man, or a god, I have yet to completely discern the difference, who is attracted to me, but not just because of how I look, and perhaps not at all for that reason. It is refreshing." She smiled.

"I am a man, in all the ways that matter, which means I have noticed how beautiful you are, strikingly so. But you are correct. I have noticed something more, and truth be told, that may be because I am a god."

"Can you tell me what that is, what you see?"

Harry took a quick look at the glassed-in control room, Frank still quite occupied. "I see a deep wisdom that, strangely, seems to be the source of a deep loneliness. And I hear an invitation."

"Am I that obvious?"

Harry smiled. "We have a talent for reading people, not unlike your own. You know that I am married, although that means little or nothing now. But my life is here on Saria, and yours on the other side of the world."

"My life for the next few days is here, and who can say where it might be in the future."

The glass door opened and Frank called from the doorway. "The pressure printouts, what are they for?"

Reluctantly, Hephaestus tore his gaze away from a look he had not seen in countless years and swallowed hard. "They track the stressor points along all the fault lines in the region. Any major quake should be apparent there long in advance, and none are really expected. Minor fluctuations in the pressure gradients seem to be the norm now, but it's still prudent to keep watch, in my view."

"This is all so fascinating," Frank said, closing the door behind him as he rejoined the others below. "Would it be possible to see the Bunker?"

"Of course," said Harry, leading the way, and considering the possibilities.

Meanwhile, Artemis provided a narrative history of Saria from its inception 20 years ago, as she strolled with Siobhan and Alice through the gardens and orchards of the main campus. She also explained the work she did as the nominal director of Mt. Olympus Security, including the years as a flight attendant with Air France, traveling the world to mobilize the remaining cells of Amazons. They met Helena Zoya when they toured the central pod, who showed them the medical facilities and described the research she did at the Fertility Institute in Boston, where Penny would continue to receive prenatal care.

As they headed to one of the neighboring pods, where Artemis knew a group of Amazons were training, Alice decided to do a little research of her own. "The Greek mythology I recall has it that you're a virgin."

Artemis laughed. "You can't believe everything you read, especially about us. But I will tell you this: I have never slept with a man. And I suspect that you can make the same claim."

Siobhan chuckled, and Alice may have blushed before adding, "Hard to keep a secret around here."

"And no reason to," Artemis responded. "Whenever I'm here, I always try to have a good time. The Amazons are quite free and open regarding matters of sex. Think about this place. It's like an all-girl boarding school, isolated from the world outside, where the students have been penned up together for 20 years."

Alice did think about it, recalling her own heady days at Mt. Holyoke.

"Besides, you've already made an impression on one very eager Amazon." Artemis smiled.

"And who would that be?" asked Alice.

"I think we both know the answer to that question... and look, there she is." Artemis was pointing to a group of six Amazons, training in the courtyard of the residential pod they had now entered.

Siobhan and Alice watched spellbound. Elaborate but ruthless defensive maneuvers, countering what appeared to be deadly cold street-fighting attacks — every move sharp and quick without ever actually landing a blow. Alice had eyes only for Cynna, who trotted over to them when the group took a break. "I was hoping to run into you," addressing Alice after an acknowledging nod to Artemis and Siobhan.

"I was about to say the same thing," Alice replied, a little flushed and flustered at the closeness of the toned young woman, dripping with what she imagined to be delicious sweat.

"Good. Then I'll see you at dinner." She gave Alice a bright smile before returning to her comrades for round two.

Alice turned to Artemis. "So, matchmaking is one of your many talents?"

She chuckled. "Just part of the Saria hospitality package."

ΩΩΩ

Four places of honor were reserved for the guests from America that evening at dinner. Penny's parents occupied the two middle chairs; the other two remained empty until Penny and Michael slipped into them, Penny by her father and Michael next to Siobhan. Alice and Marisol had begged off to sit with Cynna and Hephaestus, respectively — which no one seemed to mind, least of all Penny, who was delighted for everyone concerned. It also gave her an opportunity to assess her father's take on what he had heard and seen, and her mother a chance to get better acquainted with Michael.

Frank could not shower enough praise on Hephaestus and his accomplishments. "His intelligence and his skill, first-rate — beyond first rate. The shielding he developed for the Bunker alone, if patented, would be worth millions. But he's not interested in money. Only justice, he says. In the end, it's all about justice. Has the word in Greek carved in the stone lintel. Looks like this." Always with a pen and a small notebook at the ready, Frank did his best to reproduce the script: δικαι.

"What do you think of that?" Penny asked.

"Well, it's certainly a noble goal. And, I suppose, it's important to work toward a goal like that, even if you can't achieve it. This cyber war — that's what you're after? Justice?"

"Both more and less than that," Penny answered thoughtfully. "Many people believe justice is simply following the law. We want to support the kind of education that encourages young people to question that belief, and all the ideas about what is good and right, brought to you by a friendly corporate sponsor or the politicians they own. We want to help create individuals of high moral character, capable of deciding for themselves what is just, and courageous enough to pursue it in their own lives, and in the communities in which they live."

"Not something that can happen overnight."

"Of course not. This is a long-term project — 20 years in the making already. Hephaestus forged us wedding rings of rose gold — flat bands, almost weightless, and engraved on the inside with an ancient Greek proverb." καλοσ χαλεπον, she wrote in Frank' notebook. "Fine things are difficult."

"A man of many talents, or should I say a god."

"So you believe me now."

Frank laughed. "What choice do we have? Aside from the fact that you're our daughter, and we've got your back, always, it's either that or the Twilight Zone."

"For a time I thought I was trapped in the Matrix." Penny giggled and kissed her father's cheek. "By the way, Michael and I have arranged a day trip to Rhodes tomorrow. We'd like for you and Mom to join us."

"Of course, honey. What about Alice and Marisol?"

"They have other plans."

Siobhan started the conversation on the other side with a question. "How was your nap?" No smirk, straight-faced.

Michael, caught off-guard, took a moment to consider possible adjectives, rejecting all those that immediately jumped to mind. "I'm sure you don't want details." An innocuous statement to stall for more time. "I suppose gratifying and restful would be a fair description." He grinned.

Raising an eyebrow and offering a sly smile, Siobhan said, "Can't ask more of a nap than that."

"Your daughter has a way of getting the most out of everything she does. I suspect that's a skill she learned from you."

"Alice warned me that you were a charmer. But there was really no need, once I understood you were the same Michael who spoke to us at Penny's graduation. I recognize the same diction, the same style of flattery."

"You're just confirming what I suggested, that Penny gets more from you than her red hair. I've been told you are an anarchist," he added, altering the course of the conversation. "And I do know what that means, and what it doesn't mean."

"You're familiar with Proudhon and Kropotkin, then."

"And Bakunin, Rudolph Rocker, Emma Goldman, and your beloved Thoreau. A half dozen Amazons who I knew died fighting with the anarchists in Spain."

"They were betrayed by the communists."

"So I've been told. I brought you a book you might find interesting." Michael handed the thick paperback to her. "Some light reading for the trip back to New Mexico."

"Murray Bookchin, *The Ecology of Freedom*. Alice told me about him, I believe. He runs the Institute for Social Ecology in Vermont."

"He did. He's been dead for about a decade now. And I was kidding about light reading. The book is dense and difficult stylistically, at least to my ear, but well worth the struggle. He offers an historical narrative that informs my own thinking about the decline of the classical vision of the good life, and offers a contemporary version of anarchism, which he calls social ecology, as the antidote."

"Will I find the blueprint for your cyber war there, including the part about looting the Kinslaw Group?" Siobhan smiled sweetly, but with a dagger's edge.

Michael chuckled. "You O'Connor women never forget a thing."

"It's the Irish in us. We have very long memories."

"But if you will permit me my own recollection, I believe it more proper to describe our plans for Kinslaw as the *liberation* of its money, to support the liberal arts."

"Touché. And thank you for the book."

Elsewhere, sleeping arrangements were being discussed. "I have a suite in the Royal Pod, but I share it with Marisol," Alice told Cynna.

"That doesn't bother me if it doesn't bother you," Cynna replied cheerfully.

For reasons Alice did not want to examine too closely, hearing those words sent a delicious chill up her spine, but her good sense, or something akin to it, prevailed. "There will be no bother at all. Marisol is going to bunk with Hephaestus; we just have to give her time to collect what she needs from the room."

"How wonderful!" Cynna exclaimed. "I'm so happy for Hephaestus. You know, rumor has it that he hasn't had proper sex since Aphrodite jilted him, like 3000 years ago."

"They were married?" Alice asked, incredulous.

"Still are, as far as I know. But she's had more lovers than 100 rabbits in heat. Poor Hephaestus believed she was the love of his life, but Aphrodite was just toying with him. He took a lot of abuse from some of the other gods until Artemis stood up for him. When she takes aim at someone, she doesn't miss. Finds a weak spot and exploits the hell out of it. You really don't want to make Artemis mad."

Across the courtyard, Harry was describing the cabin he had designed and built himself to Marisol. She put her hand on his arm, a flirty gesture, and looked him square in the eyes. "How big is the bed? That is what I really want to know." She smiled.

"Big enough," he said. "It's not like I haven't considered something like this."

"From what I hear, that is all you have been doing — considering — for a very long time."

"That's true." he sighed, "which is why I'm a little bit nervous."

"It is not like this is an everyday sort of thing for me, you know. Most men, especially in Puerto Rico, are scared of a woman like me, a woman who can look into their hearts. The fact that you are just nervous — that is a good sign." She smiled.

Nervous or not, Hephaestus had never felt this kind of attraction, this kind of desire, not even with Aphrodite. That had been a foolish enchantment, literally. He had been seduced by her beauty, her siren's wiles, and his own imagination, his image of ideal love. Marisol had depth and substance; there was nothing ephemeral or illusory about her. Here was an opportunity to experience something real, and he was not going to squander it. The future could take care of itself. "So, what now?" he asked.

"I will grab a toothbrush. You get the ATV, and pick me up at the entrance to the Royal Pod."

When he pulled up, she was waiting with her duffle, no doubt stuffed with all her belongings. "I'm being presumptuous, I know. I hope you do not mind," she said with a wry smile.

"Not at all. Feel free to presume whatever you like."

ΩΩΩ

Hermes stood next to the gleaming white Airbus 145 helicopter, *Mt. Olympus Tours,* discreetly stenciled on the side in blue, as Michael, Penny, and her parents made their way up the small hill just northeast of the main campus. Penny had wanted her folks to get a taste of the tourist experience — this being their first trip to Europe, let alone the Greek Islands. To complement their beach time at Diafani, Michael suggested a trip to Rhodes, which had a wealth of historical sites dating back at least to the 8th century BC, and a cosmopolitan cultural milieu. He had consulted with Hermes, who told him the only way to make a day trip there would be by helicopter. The plan was to fly to the city of Rhodes, which would have them sightseeing in about an hour and a half, the flight itself taking less than an hour. If there was time, they could stop at Lindos on the way back.

Michael offered a brief narrative of the history of Rhodes on the flight over. "Because of its location, Rhodes became an important player in trade throughout the eastern Mediterranean, generating a lot of wealth but also making it a target for conquest, each invading power leaving its mark. The Persians came in 490 BC and held the island for over a decade before being dislodged by forces of the Athenian League. Rhodes more or less maintained its autonomy for the next half-century until the Romans arrived in 164. When the Roman Empire divided, Rhodes became a province of the eastern Byzantine Empire and remained so until the island was occupied by the Knights of St. John, retreating Crusaders, who built the walled city which today is known as the Old Town, the oldest continuously inhabited medieval town in Europe, and our first stop. Some 200 years later, the Ottoman Turks took control and held it for about four centuries. The Italians ruled for a brief time between the World Wars, after which Rhodes and the rest of the Dodecanese Islands, including Karpathos and Saria, were returned to Greece.

"Rhodes achieved early fame for the Colossus of Rhodes, one of the so-called Seven Wonders of the Ancient World. It was a huge bronze statue of Helios, about the height of your Statute of Liberty, completed in 280 BC, after over a decade of construction. Unfortunately, it was completely destroyed by an earthquake in 226 BC. Just so you know, Helios was thought to be the Sun God, but in fact did not exist. On the other hand, the sun itself was real and remains so."

Hermes set down the helicopter on the ferry dock. He closed it up while his passengers loaded into a shuttle for the short trip to the Old Town. They stood before two stout round turreted towers, ramparts on the top of each, a frieze carved into the stone between them, resting above a narrow gateway. "This is called the St. Catherine's Gate," said Michael. "There are 11 such gates or entrances through the wall. This is my favorite — fortification as art."

"Is that St. Catherine in the middle of the relief there?" asked Siobhan.

"I'm told it's the Virgin Mary, flanked by St. John and St. Peter, but I'm not an expert on Christian iconography. Let's go in. We could all use some breakfast, and I have an errand to run for Athena on Sokratous Street."

Michael led them to the far eastern flank of Hippokratous Square, Rhodes Old Town's bustling main square brimming with open-air restaurants, selecting one directly across from the Castellania, a fourteenth-century structure built by the Knights of St. John. He suggested a traditional Greek breakfast of graviera cheese omelets, *galatopita* (milk pie), *tiganites* (pancakes), protein-rich and starchy, based on the eating habits of the early Greeks, who needed a hearty breakfast to see them through a day of hard work. They all carried water and sunscreen, and Michael had also packed a supply of protein bars and fruit for later.

Penny marveled at Michael's knowledge of the local history and his command of the day. Of course, he might have easily witnessed much of the history first hand. Her parents, usually so inquisitive, sometimes aggressively so, were for the most part deferential, content to listen and learn. They seemed quite comfortable following Michael's lead and, along with Penelope herself, acutely aware of the need as visitors to show due respect to the culture of their hosts.

While they ate, Michael pointed out a few architectural features of the Castellania, including the early Renaissance character of the window openings on the semi-open-air arcade, dominating the first floor. "The lesser officials of the Order of Knights had offices off the arcade on the ground floor. The second floor, reached by that external staircase, originally housed courtrooms and jail cells. The Ottomans turned the whole place into a mosque, and it's now a public library and archive."

"Why no handrail on the stairs?" asked Frank, always the engineer.

"It's typical of the period. My best guess is that external stairs usually accessed parapets and would be used by soldiers carrying bulky weapons. Stairways inside public buildings of this era always had balustrades."

After breakfast, they headed west on Sokratous, the main shopping street, a narrow cobblestone pedestrian way lined with shops and open bazaars. Siobhan and Penny lingered here and there, admiring fabrics, colors, and designs. Frank was polite but clearly anxious to see the ancient Acropolis. For his part, Michael was searching for a particular shop described by Athena, where he would find Hermes standing out front if things had gone according to plan. And there he was, a big shopping bag hanging from one hand.

"Everything alright?" asked Michael.

"All good," Hermes replied. "They're quite beautiful. Bought one for myself off the rack."

Penny, curious as ever, intervened. "What are you two talking about?"

"Wedding clothes," said Michael. "Athena special-ordered tunics for me and her brother. You'll see them tomorrow." He gave her his sweetest smile.

Penny scowled briefly but accepted the fairness of that; Michael had yet to see her dress.

"I'll see you back at the dock," said Hermes.

Michael nodded. "Three hours, maybe a little less."

They shook hands and Hermes retreated back down Sokratous.

Before leaving the walled Old Town, Michael led them to the ruins of the Temple of Aphrodite, dating back to the third century BC, and the Grand Masters Palace, originally built by the Knights, but destroyed by a gunpowder explosion in the nineteenth century, and restored by the Italians in the early twentieth century. It now serves as a museum, including artifacts from the Christian and Ottoman periods. They exited via the D'Amboise Gate, the most massively fortified of all the gates, built by the Grand Master D'Amboise in 1512, barely a decade before the Ottomans finally breached the walls.

The Acropolis of Rhodes, dating from the fifth century BC, was their next stop. There they strolled among a variety of ruins, including the partially restored ruins of the Temple of Athena and Zeus, a stately temple dominated by Doric columned porticos on all sides, and the smaller and less complete Temple of Apollo. Nearby was the Odeon, a restored marble amphitheater with curved benched seating for 800 rising gently up a hillside from the stage, and a partially restored athletic stadium, stretching some 70 yards in length. Frank especially was overawed by the technical expertise and the labor required to produce such structures so long ago. His curiosity could no longer be contained, and Michael patiently answered his questions as best he could, noting at one point that "the temples were built *for* us, not *by* us," which produced a good-natured chuckle.

By the time they returned to the helicopter, it was late afternoon, and the consensus was to just take a peek at Lindos from the air on the way back to Saria. After all, the wedding was the next day, and Athena, taskmaster that she was, wanted Michael and Penny awake well before dawn.

CHAPTER 8

Gray dawn. Actually a generous description, as there was barely enough light to see the path as Michael and Penny made their way down to the cove, hand in hand, only half awake. She could just make out the outlines of the shade sails covering the back half of the beach — black in this light, but all different hues of blue, like the Mediterranean, when they flew overhead yesterday afternoon. Farther down, near the water's edge, she saw a soft swirling white light surrounding the faint images of their fellow travelers, Marisol and Hephaestus.

"Michael, do you see that?" she gasped, squeezing his hand. "It's like our first night."

"What?" he asked.

"The light, the swirling light."

Michael chuckled. "New love, no doubt. Your sight is better than mine now, remember?"

She did, with a twinge of sadness, perhaps guilt. All that he had given up for her. But then her eyes teared, recalling that moment when he had told her how easy it had been, for the love of Penelope, and she leaned up and kissed his cheek.

Hugs all around as the two couples met. "What's in the trunk?" Penny asked.

"Wedding clothes," Hephaestus replied. "We'll all change on the boat."

"Where are we going, anyway?" Penny pressed, curious and persistent as ever.

"That depends. We'll let Ares explain," he said, pointing to the single-mast catamaran gliding swiftly toward them.

Penny turned to Michael, wide-eyed, "Ares?"

Michael smiled. "The one and only. Father of the Amazons."

Hephaestus and Michael loaded the trunk on board the sleek 40-foot cat, while Ares addressed the two women on the beach. Penny had a hard time imagining him as the God of War. He had the build for it, like Michelangelo's David, but his face framed by soft dark curls, had the look of a cherub or an innocent preadolescent child. And yet, he spoke with the formality of a judge.

"I have listened with keen interest to the testimony of four Olympians — Athena, Hephaestus, Artemis, and Apollo, hereafter to be known by me as Michael — as to your unusual abilities, as well as your unfailing courage and loyalty. My own eyes now confirm what I have been told. I have also been advised by Themis, Regent of the Amazons, speaking on behalf of all my children, that they would be honored to admit you to their ranks. At this point, the choice is yours."

Penny could not quite believe what she was hearing. To be acknowledged as an Amazon would be her fanciful dream realized. She turned in stunned silent desperation to Marisol.

Marisol smiled at Penny and spoke boldly to Ares. "I am flattered to be offered such distinction, but can accept only if by so doing I accompany Penelope, the one truly worthy, but who is at the moment too overcome to speak. Perhaps she might be allowed to nod, for both of us."

Ares laughed. "Of course."

Penny nodded, as if a little girl offered an ice cream cone, and recovering herself, bowed her head with gracious deference.

"Then we shall sail with haste to the secret shrine of the Amazon Queens. There you shall be initiated as the sun rises, and then as commanded by Athena, with the blessing of the bride, Michael and Penelope will exchange vows, witnessed only by Hephaestus and Marisol."

ΩΩΩ

The wedding party assembled on the squared-off bow of the catamaran, salt spray cooling their bare feet, as Ares motored slowly toward the beach where the blue-shaded space awaited, now occupied by Olympians, Amazons, and Penny's family. Penelope stood tall and proud on Michael's arm, a ridiculous grin on her face, waves of her red locks dancing about. She was wearing the cream-colored halter neck dress tailored for her by Alice and Marisol — a simple design, but quite elegant, with a tight antique lace bodice above a mid-calf flowing full skirt, with wide pleats, belted at the waist by a silken tasseled rope. Marisol, standing to her left, wore the same style dress in pale yellow, but without the lace, her long black hair tied back. The men, including Ares at the helm and Hephaestus to Michael's right, wore the narrow V-neck tunics ordered by Athena above traditional fishermen's pants — loose-fitting, off-white, and tied at the waist and above the ankles. The tunics were all elaborately embroidered around the neck, the slits framed by crossing patterns of various designs. Michael had crossed oars of white thread on a field of Greek blue, Hephaestus black hammers on gold, and Ares silver spears on blood red.

As the boat edged ever closer, Penny clearly spied Athena standing between what appeared to be two huge tuning forks made of wood driven into the sand, the tines of one narrow and the other opened wide, and both stems festooned with garlands of colorful flowers. Athena herself looked every bit the Greek goddess, all in white, a sleeveless free-flowing blouse, rippling in the gentle breeze, and a narrow-pleated ankle-length skirt with a chunky woven pewter belt. Her feet were bare, as were everyone's, or so it seemed.

The twin hulls of the catamaran ground to a halt in the sand a few feet from the water's edge. Michael lifted the hinged section of railing, folding it back, and stepped down into the shallows, helping first Penny and then Marisol to do the same. Hephaestus joined them and the two couples sloshed to shore and headed toward the shaded shelter, arm in arm, Michael and Penny in the fore. The crowd rose, applauding. Directed to a bench in front by Athena, Penny broke ranks briefly to kiss her parents and her aunt, and to scratch Sappho behind the ears, before taking her place between Michael and Marisol.

Athena addressed the multitude, in her firm commanding voice: "Everyone is present now, save one — a representative from Mt. Olympus, bearing a special gift."

Audible gasps filled the air as Ares, having tossed an anchor from the stern of his boat, waded through the rising tide, an ancient oar slung over his shoulder. He placed the oar in the two garland-wrapped posts, obviously designed for this purpose. "The Oar of Odysseus!" he called out, to gasps louder and more universal. "A gift to Saria from Poseidon, to be used as an altar in today's ceremony, and hereafter to be kept by the Amazons, as a symbol of the unwavering support of the work being done here in defense of the values of Mt. Olympus.

"Most of you know the story of the Oar as told by Homer. According to that version, the blind prophet Teiresias instructed Odysseus, as an act of penance, to walk inland with the Oar until he reached a people so unfamiliar with the sea that they would see the Oar as a winnowing fan. This after he had been away from Ithaca and his beloved Penelope for 20 years. Those of us who knew Odysseus tell a different tale. He had the character of a wanderer, and despite the authenticity of his love for Penelope, he simply could not stay home for long. For us, and even in Homer's *Odyssey*, Penelope proves herself the real hero, steadfast in the love of her husband and in defense of her self-respect, her honor, and her home. Our Penelope and her friend Marisol have displayed the same qualities of courage and loyalty, and today, with the breaking dawn, they were initiated by me, with the blessing of the sisters of the tribe, into the order of the Amazons. They, of course, cannot call me father but, at Penelope's suggestion, their god... father."

Ares, hearing a few polite chuckles, turned to Athena. "Tough crowd," he said, producing the cathartic laughs he sought.

Smiling, he continued. "The elder Olympians — Zeus, Hera, Poseidon, Demeter, and Hestia — have chosen not to attend the ceremony today for fear that their absence from Mt. Olympus would be noticed by my troubled sister, Aphrodite, or one of her many spies, thereby compromising the identity and location of she whom they have pledged to defend. Their absence should be understood in this light as a prudent exercise of their duty to Penelope and those she loves. I have been sent in their stead to wish Michael and Penelope much happiness in their love, and all of us success in the coming war. I will step aside now, as I am always honored to do, to hear the wisdom of Athena."

Athena, who had been standing to one side, assumed a position behind the Oar and took command. "We are gathered here today because of a prophecy, proclaimed by the Oracle at Delphi some 2,800 years ago. I believe that ancient prophecy will be fulfilled shortly after the winter sun begins to rise in the southern sky. Most of us believe this, because the two most intimately involved believe it, and we believe them. How could we not?

"But notwithstanding the truth of the prophecy, Fate has brought us together. We stand today on the Island of Saria, home of the Amazons, on the brink of a mighty undertaking, because Michael and his noble sister Artemis revived interest in the prophecy and its potential 20 years ago. Together, they energized the effort that has created this home, and a future with hope, for the Olympians, the Amazons, and the whole of the Western world, if not the planet itself. True or not, we celebrate today the opportunity thus created, and consummate our commitment to it.

"As wedding celebrations go, this one will be rather unique. There will be no giving of the bride — a significant departure from tradition for two important reasons. First, Penelope and Michael have given themselves to each other...." Hearing a few snickers from the galley, Athena turned her most forbidding stare on Cynna, a likely suspect. "Yes, in that way — but in other profound, mysterious, and even perilous ways. Few have the courage to risk everything, to bare their souls to each other as these two have. A bond of incredible strength and durability has already been forged. They are married in all essential respects save one — and that we will rectify right now. Will the wedding party stand and come forward?"

Athena directed Michael and Hephaestus to her left, Penny and Marisol to her right. "Greek law requires that marriage vows be witnessed by at least two individuals. My understanding is that Penelope and Michael exchanged vows in the presence of Hephaestus and Marisol, who have sworn on their honor to guard the sanctity of the promises made, and to guarantee so far as they are able their faithful observance. Do you, Hephaestus, so testify?"

"I do."

"Do you, Marisol, likewise testify?"

"I do."

Athena looked out at the assembled guests with a sly smile. "Has a nice ring to it, don't you think?"

Marisol and Hephaestus squirmed and blushed, Penny giggled, and Athena acknowledged the quiet laughter of the crowd with a slight bow of her head. Looking very pleased with herself, she turned to Hephaestus and Marisol. "Rings?" she asked, smiling.

Hephaestus glared at his sister as he handed her the ring in his charge; Marisol kept a lower profile as she proffered the other. Holding both firmly in her fist, Athena whispered a Greek blessing, then held her fist aloft. "By the power vested in me, I solemnly declare that, with the giving and receiving of these rings, Penelope and Michael shall be legally married, with all the attending rights of citizenship to follow." She opened her fist to Michael, then to Penelope, and stood back.

Michael took Penny's hand and slipped on the rose gold band, whispering "καλοσ χαλεπον." Whispering "καλοσ χαλεπον," Penny did the same, and then they kissed.

Athena allowed the applause that followed to recede. "Before beginning the second part of this service, and perhaps the more important, I will ask one more task of this couple: to lift what I regard as the curse of the Oar — the energy within it that enticed a soul as wise as Odysseus to wander far and wide, forsaking the company of his beloved wife."

Placing their hands on the Oar and gazing into each other's eyes, Michael began. "Whatever path Fate leads me down, I will take you with me".... "and I will go willingly, as I did that first night we were together," rejoined Penny. The couple removed their hands, returning to their seats, joined again by Hephaestus and Marisol.

"By the love of Penelope and Michael, at home always with each other, I proclaim the curse of the Oar discharged, granting it a home on Saria, never again to wander. And we may trust all who lay their hands upon this Oar to know Saria as their home, no matter where they might be.

"I come now to the second reason why this ceremony eschewed a giving of the bride. Traditionally, such an act represents the giving of a woman from one family to another. Here, instead, we have a need to merge two families: on the one hand, the Olympians and their defenders, the Amazons, which now formally include Penelope and Marisol; on the other hand, Penelope's American family. The stakes are high indeed.

"There is an immediate need to protect Penelope and those she loves from the misguided designs of Aphrodite. We need not seek allegiance in this regard, for everyone here is bound by love and honor to this end. But the coming war requires an abiding commitment. All of us must don the mantle of warriors, for whom loyalty and courage are sacred, to have any chance of restoring the values of Mt. Olympus to their proper place. Therefore, I ask Penelope to invite her family to come forward and join us, by placing their hands upon the Oar, and to know from this day forward, a home in Saria."

Penny rose and approached her family, who stood in turn to receive her. No words needed to be spoken, as Penny turned to lead them forward, halted by Sappho's sharp bark. Penny smiled down at the red-haired dog, then knelt to pick her up. As they made their way to the Oar, everyone rose. Penny placed Sappho's paw upon the Oar, followed in turn by her mother, her father, and her aunt. Cheers filled the quiet cove of Saria, and tears Athena's eyes.

ΩΩΩ

Travel day. The first to leave would be Penny's parents and her aunt, with Sappho, of course. Siobhan had decided that she and Frank would remain with Alice in Boston for a few days. As she had explained to Penny, "My sister and I want to make sure your father understands exactly what he has agreed to and is completely on board." Marisol had decided to remain behind on Saria. She, Helena Zoya, and Artemis would meet up with the honeymooners in Sicily 17 days hence, and return to Boston from there. She and Penny were at the moment watching Hermes and Cynna, who was also returning to Boston, stow the last of the luggage on the helicopter for the short flight to Karpathos Airport, where the Gulfstream sat fueled and ready.

"What did Athena mean by the rights of citizenship yesterday?" Marisol asked.

"That was a reminder to my father of why they were dragged all the way here for the wedding. Because I married a Greek citizen on Greek soil, I am entitled to claim Greek citizenship. Both Michael and I will then be dual citizens, as will any children we have, wherever they are born. Thinking ahead, are you?" Penny smiled knowingly.

"Not you, too," groused Marisol.

"I saw the light."

"What does that mean?"

"I'll tell you on the flight back to Boston."

Not really anxious to pursue that line of conversation further, Marisol changed tack. "When do you and Michael leave?"

"After my folks are in the air. It's seven hours or so to Santorini, depending on the wind, so we'll spend the night on the boat. Ares is going to teach me how to sail, so it could take a lot longer." Penny giggled.

"So Santorini and then Florence?"

"Five nights in Santorini and seven in Florence. Two nights in Athens in between. We can't get to Italy from the Santorini, and I really should see the Athenian Acropolis. I am a classics student, after all."

"I think you are wise not to try to see too much."

"My first impulse was to see Europe in 17 days. Then Greece and Italy in 17 days. But I realized that this will be the first time Michael and I have to ourselves, except for the Amazons lurking about, of course. We have our place in Cambridge, but you and my aunt are right upstairs — not that I'm complaining about that." Penny hastened to add.

"I know what you mean," said Marisol, nodding. "I am glad that Harry's place is relatively isolated, away from the main compound. What I do not understand is Sicily."

Penny laughed. "That's another story for the trip back to Boston."

"I hope I'm not interrupting," said Hephaestus, who had climbed the hill from the campus behind them unnoticed, carrying a polished wooden box. Marisol just beamed with delight, her joy immediate and palpable.

"Of course not," Penny said, feeling a little envious of her friend's good fortune. She had been denied the excitement and the simple pleasures of new love. Her relationship with Michael had been fraught with danger and difficulties from the beginning and colored by the need for deception. Much of that was behind them now, and she was cheered by the promise of two carefree weeks alone with Michael. Besides, she was genuinely happy for Marisol. She smiled. "What's in the box?"

"Something for you," he said, placing the box on the bench next to her. "Think of it as a wedding gift, if you like, but it's really a thank you for bringing this one to me." A hand extended found Marisol's, and he gently pulled her up from the bench, holding her at his side. "Open it."

Penny lifted the close- fitting lid revealing a stack of metal plates, glinting gold and red in the noonday sun, meticulously engraved with narrow lines of Greek, like her wedding band. She looked up, her question unspoken.

"It's a journal of sorts. I started it when Aphrodite left me, and once every decade or so, I engraved my reflections. I experimented with the metal, rose gold like your rings, but with variable amounts of copper. The plates are numbered, but with the letters of the Greek alphabet; we didn't have numbers back then. There are two series, 48 plates in all, covering about 500 years. Marisol told me you are starting a graduate program in classics. I thought you might find these interesting."

"Wow. Are you sure? I mean, some of this must be... personal."

"That time is well behind me now. It documents the era historians today refer to as Archaic, when much of the mythology surrounding the gods was propagated. You might glean some valuable insights, and if, as I assume, you share your findings with Marisol, it might provide her with a deeper understanding of me. Michael and Artemis can help you translate."

Penny replaced the lid, stood, and kissed Hephaestus on the cheek. "Thank you," she said, not for the first time.

ΩΩΩ

Penny had never experienced such luxury. They hadn't left their private Santorini villa for three days. From bedroom to balcony and back again, with occasional dips in their private pool and stops in the well-stocked kitchen for fresh fruit, local cheeses, olives, humus, *daktyla*, and other goodies. Breakfast and dinner, ordered from the hotel restaurant below, was delivered as the sun rose in the morning and set in the evening, to be consumed on the balcony, from which the views were spectacular.

Sitting in an area carved out of the topmost cliff of the caldera, they could see the whole of the crater, the giant hole filled with seawater, surrounding the black lava islands, Nea Kamini and Palia Kamini, home to a sleeping volcano that last erupted in 1956. Across the bay was the inhabited island of Thirasia, actually the other rim of the volcano. About two miles south of Fira, Santorini's capital, their villa also overlooked Porto Athinaos, the main ferry port, where many of the cruise ships also anchored in the morning. Boat watching over breakfast, and to accompany dinner, magnificent sunsets, rivaling the best Santa Fe had to offer.

As they were finishing breakfast on the fourth day, between sips of her ginger tea, Penny waved her hand, an encompassing gesture. "All this must cost a fortune."

Michael smiled. "Not as much as you might think. This place, the hotel below — in fact, our honeymoon accommodations in Florence as well — are owned by Mt. Olympus Resorts. Lost revenue, to be sure, but a minor blip in the bottom line, of no real consequence to the elder Olympians. Our wedding gift from them."

"Should I send them a thank you note?" Penny smirked.

"Honestly? They feel a need to thank you. When it's safe, we'll travel to Mt. Olympus and introduce them to our daughter. That will be thanks enough, trust me." Michael swallowed the last of his coffee. "How would you feel about a day at the beach, with a detour perhaps, to visit the lost city of Atlantis?"

"Atlantis?" she asked, incredulous.

"Sort of." Michael's cryptic reply.

Penny slathered herself in sunscreen while Michael packed a picnic lunch, and soon they were heading south in a sporty red Porsche Boxster convertible, followed by a more sedate Land Rover carrying two of their four Amazon guardians. They stopped briefly in Perissa to view the expansive black sand beach there, then traveled on to the Akrotiri excavation site.

On the drive down, Michael had explained that the Akrotiri ruins were of a Bronze Age Minoan settlement, thought to be second in size to the Minoan site at Knossos on Crete. It had been buried in volcanic ash in 1627 BC, and like the Roman ruins of Pompeii, was remarkably well preserved. Some historians believe that word of a lost Minoan city reached Plato and inspired his story of Atlantis in the *Timaeus*.

Penny found the actual ruins to be quite impressive. Three-story buildings, paved streets, an elaborate drainage system, as well as photographs of beautiful frescos, quality pottery, and copper processing tools removed to an off-site museum, all spoke of a highly advanced and sophisticated civilization. She peppered Michael with questions, most of which he deflected with the disingenuous sounding claim, "before my time." She resolved to probe the source of his reluctance, but only after lunch. She was hungry, always hungry.

They walked with their picnic basket partway down the access path to the Red Beach. Because of the danger of slides from the blood-red cliffs, they found a sheltered spot where they could eat their lunch with a view of the high cliffs and the narrow beach of red sand below. Penny had never seen anything comparable, but she was somewhat distracted by the wonderful smells and tastes of the *gyros* Michael had made. She managed to savor both the view and the food, and once sated turned her most determined stare on Michael. "So what don't you want to tell me about the Minoan civilization?"

"You're not going to let this go, are you?"

Penny smiled. "Have I ever?"

"Alright," he sighed. "But let's get to Vlychada first. We can play a little in the water. Lounge under the straw umbrellas. And I'll tell you what you want to know."

Michael was right about the beach. Lengthy and not crowded at all. The backdrop of white cliffs, sculpted from the volcanic rock like fingers by wind and sand and water, standing straight up, was stunning. The sand, more gray than black, and the water warm and crystal clear. She let him lead her out into the sea, maybe a hundred feet from shore, where they could bob with the incoming swells. Like a gentle massage.

After 40 minutes or so, they returned to the beach, finding a pair of shaded lounge chairs away from the tourists. Clouds had moved in, blocking the sun, but the heat radiating from the sand was enough to warm them. They laid on their sides facing each other, and Michael told her his tale.

"The Minoans created the first truly European civilization, dating back to around 3000 BC. It flourished until about 1600 BC before declining rapidly. You'll recall what Athena said about the origins and fadings of immortals — a good answer, I thought, to the spirit of the question asked. But she might have been more forthcoming about the specific origins of the Olympians, the first generation of which were in fact the children of the Minoan gods. My elders supplanted their parents and grandparents by helping to create the Mycenaean civilization, the first iteration of what we now call Western civilization, which hastened the decline of the Minoans. My mother, Leto, was a lesser Minoan deity. There is a shrine to her on Crete to this day. But by the time Artemis and I were born, she was a mere shadow of herself. In a manner of speaking, my father, and my aunts and uncles, and even her own children, helped to kill her. It is not a history I like to think about."

"You were just a child, Michael. Civilizations grow old and die. And in my world, now yours as well, parents grow old and die."

Michael smiled. "There is another implication to consider here. Our daughter, and any other children we have — and perhaps Marisol's children, if Fate is kind to Hephaestus and her — may supplant us as authors of a new civilization."

"If that be their destiny, let us hope they do a better job than us," said Penny.

Their final day on Santorini began as a touristy affair. After an early breakfast, they took the Porsche to Oia, hoping to beat the crowds. Perhaps the most picturesque village in all of Greece, sitting atop an impressive cliff with spectacular views, the once quiet counter-culture community was now anything but quiet. They wandered the maze of narrow streets, full of whitewashed homes, shops and cafes with blue shutters, art galleries, and blue-domed churches until the crowds became unbearable. Then they climbed down the long, zigzagging steps to Ammoudi Bay for a fresh seafood lunch at the water's edge. That was enough for Penny. They returned to their villa for a little love in the afternoon, followed by a light dinner, a final sunset, and an early bedtime — early enough that they actually got a good night's sleep.

ΩΩΩ

She would never feel comfortable with all this extravagance. That was Penny's first thought when she awoke in the luxurious hotel suite in Florence. Of course, she was lying next to Michael, who was still asleep, and that felt right and proper. Besides, he had told her for the umpteenth time that it was all a gift from her in-laws, and she should simply enjoy it. She did love the central location, overlooking the Arno River, a stone's throw from the *Ponte Vecchio*, the famous pedestrian bridge lined with shops.

They had walked that bridge their first day in Florence, and Michael had recounted some of its history for her. The original stone shops had been included in the design of the fourteenth-century structure in order to help pay for it. The Butchers Guild came to dominate trade on the bridge in the fifteenth century and held sway until banished in the late sixteenth century by the ruling Medici family because of the stench. By the seventeenth century, the quaint chaos of shops apparent today had taken shape, as the new tradesmen built upward and out over the river.

Penny found the *Ponte Vecchio* charming. In fact, she found the whole atmosphere of Florence more congenial than the Athenian Acropolis. But she didn't know why, especially given her mind's inclination toward analysis and the elegant logic of mathematics. And as a student of classics, she had longed to visit the Acropolis. Sitting in the middle of the Parthenon, however, she had felt oddly detached. Perhaps, she thought at the time, the orderliness, the austere control of space, did not speak to her as a woman. While she still entertained that belief, it really only begged the question: why? Now, finding herself in the epicenter of the Renaissance, surrounded by the work of its greatest artists, she was feeling her way toward an answer.

For starters, she knew it was not about misogyny. There was more than enough of that to go around in Classical Greece and Renaissance Italy, to say nothing of her own times. Neither was it about the mathematics. Filippo Brunelleschi's dome for the Florence Cathedral was an engineering feat of genius, and the use of linear perspective in Renaissance painting and architecture was equal to the subtle use of curvature in the Parthenon — the slight bulging of the Doric columns, for example — to enhance the appearance rather than the reality of geometrical precision.

Much of the art she was seeing in Florence was religiously themed — not surprising, given that the Church often commissioned the work. But the Renaissance artists produced work that celebrated the human form and displayed genuine human emotions. Unlike the didactic or instructive character of earlier religious art that invited contemplation, the effect of this new art was immediate and concrete. Penny could relate to it; she was moved.

The Parthenon appealed to her intellect, her ability to analyze and abstract. That was an important part of who she was, but now she was more in touch with her body. She thought about the distinction she had drawn between fucking and making love and the feelings of detachment she had felt while engaged in the former — similar to the feeling she had experienced in the Parthenon. And she was pregnant now, in direct and definitive relationship with the life growing inside her.

She looked at Michael sleeping beside her in the bed and felt a warm rush wash over her. God, she loved that man! His dream of ennobling the individual through the liberal arts was the right approach, for the liberal arts build character — and character unites, or rather requires, both the abstract and the concrete. A person of high character has principles to live by, but responds to the actual conditions with care and compassion. Justice tempered by mercy, where mercy is not understood as bestowed, but woven into the very fabric of moral judgment. That is the ethical life, the classical vision of the good life.

The Parthenon was meant to inspire transcendence, the contemplation of something akin to Plato's forms. But such forms, even if of the good or the beautiful, are sterile, she thought, because they are entirely abstract. They do not account for the feminine, the contextual, the life-giving forces of care and compassion. Renaissance art, on the other hand, embodies such forces, directing attention to the human experience and insisting on its importance. Michael stirred, and Penny giggled, anxious to share with him the somewhat ironic conclusion that the religious art of the Renaissance was less in tune with the transcendent purpose of religion than classical paganism.

ΩΩΩ

A cool Tuscan morning greeted Michael and Penny as they strolled hand in hand to the *Piazza della Signoria*, early enough to beat the heat and the crowds. This was their third visit, and Penny was feeling oddly jaded. The replica of Michelangelo's David standing in front of the *Palazzo Vecchio* still caught her eye, but not like the original in the *Galleria dell'Accademia*. Some of the remaining statuary in the *Piazza* appealed to her artistic sensibilities, especially Cellini's Perseus and Medusa and Giambologna's Rape of the Sabines, but she had tired of the ostentatious display of power and violence no doubt intended to glorify the Medici, who had commissioned most of the work while holding the secular reins of power in Florence.

Fortunately, they were just passing through the *Piazza* on their way to the *Galleria degli Uffizi* to view the extraordinary collection of Renaissance paintings. Penny was surprised by what they saw first, works from the seventeenth century by Caravaggio, El Greco, Velazques, Rubens, Rembrandt, and van Dyck. The mood of most of these paintings was somber, not the celebratory and liberating spirit she had expected to see.

"You have a good eye," Michael told her. "These paintings are post-Renaissance, probably classified by art historians as Baroque. What you want is upstairs."

Michael was right. On the second floor, the full flower of Florentine and Italian Renaissance painting was on display, spanning the fifteenth and early sixteenth centuries, including works by Leonardo da Vinci, Raphael, Michelangelo, Filippo Lippi, Piero della Francesca, Paolo Uccello, and Parmigianino, as well as a large number of paintings by

Sandro Botticelli. Penny was drawn to the Madonnas, by Lippi, Parmigianino, and especially Raphael — perhaps for obvious reasons. But she was most fascinated by da Vinci's unfinished Adoration of the Magi, recalling Michelangelo's four unfinished sculptures in the Hall of Prisoners at the *Galleria dell'Accademia*. Art in progress was like life, she thought, underway but still full of possibilities.

Then there was the Birth of Venus by Botticelli, probably the most well-known painting in the entire *Uffizi* collection — Venus being Aphrodite's Roman name. It depicts the goddess emerging from the sea fully grown, being blown to shore on a giant scallop shell. Botticelli relied on the prevailing myth of Aphrodite's genesis dating back to Hesiod, as arising solely from the castrated genitals of Uranus, which had been tossed into the sea by Cronus. Homer offered an alternative account in the *Iliad*, where Aphrodite is described as the daughter of Zeus and Dione. Penny, aware of both stories, and standing before the Botticelli, took the occasion to quiz Michael about what was true.

"I know nothing about Aphrodite's birth first-hand," he said. "But, as I've told you, the first generation of Olympians were direct descendants of the Minoan gods. Hesiod's tales of primordial gods and Titans are all a product of his imagination, nothing more than a creation myth. So, no Uranus, no Cronus. There was a Dione, probably Aphrodite's mother, but that's where the story gets murky.

"Dione, like my mother, Leto, was a Minoan goddess, who eventually faded from existence. Her name, however, suggests a goddess of some importance. In Archaic Greek, Dios is synonymous with Zeus, and Dione is its feminine form. The Minoans worshipped above all the Great Goddess. I believe, based upon her name, probably a name given her by Zeus, that Dione was that goddess, and in all likelihood, Zeus's mother. If, as Homer suggests, Aphrodite is the daughter of Zeus and Dione, she would be the product of an incestuous coupling, which could help explain her psychopathology. It makes political sense to me that when Zeus seized power, he would have claimed the Great Goddess as his consort. But it is not something he is willing to talk about."

Penny's eyes got big, and under her breath she whispered, "Holy shit."

ΩΩΩ

The *Museo Nazionale del Bargello* was the last art venue on Penny's list. The building itself was one of the oldest in Florence, dating back to 1255. They entered on the ground floor and immediately found themselves in a gallery featuring four works by Michelangelo in marble: an early Bacchus, a bas-relief of the Madonna with Child, a mature bust of Brutus, and the David-Apollo. The last of these was unfinished and, apparently, Michelangelo's intention was unknown — thus, the double name. Because the sculpture looked nothing like Michael, Penny concluded with a giggle that it must be an early rendering of David.

They made their way to the central courtyard and up the stairs to the main hall, with a beautiful high vaulted ceiling and dominated by the works of Donatello. Penny had already seen examples of his work, a copy of the bronze Judith and Holofernes in the *Piazza della Signoria*, and the Penitent Magdalene, ragged and emaciated, in the *Museo dell'Opera del Duomo*. But she had been particularly keen on seeing his bronze David, the first known free-standing nude statue produced since ancient times, and often considered the first major work of Renaissance sculpture. She found the pose to be a lyrical, almost playful rendering, complete with a Tuscan shepherd's hat. There was a second bronze piece, Amore Atys, again playful, as if dancing, a silly grin on his boyish face. Atys, a Phrygian shepherd boy, had some connection to Cybele in Greek mythology — at least so far as Penny could determine. In addition to the two striking bronze figures, there were several Donatello works in marble: an early David she found stiff and uninteresting, a more impressive St. George, and the original *Marzocco* — the Florentine lion holding the town's crest in its paw, removed from the battlements of *Palazzo Vecchio*.

Back down in the courtyard, Penny saw a sign directing patrons to the temporary exhibit of Apollo and Daphne, by Gian Lorenzo Bernini, on loan from the *Galleria Borghese* in Rome. The photograph of the marble sculpture was stunning. "Let's go see!" said Penny excitedly.

Michael pressed his lips together in a tight line, grim-faced. "You go ahead. I'll wait here."

Puzzled by his reaction, Penny asked, "What's the matter?" Met with silence, she continued. "The subject matter? I don't believe for one second that you would have ever lusted after a 12-year-old girl, let alone tried to rape her."

"It's not that. Something that's hard for me to talk about. You go. I know the work. It really is quite beautiful."

Penny was stumped. Ever since their walk in Cambridge, Michael had never refused to talk to her, to hold back. But she could see the pain clearly etched on his face. She would give him some time alone, some space to work through whatever had upset him, to consider her feelings as well as his own. She leaned up and kissed his cheek. "Ok. I'll be right back."

The sculpture was beautiful, the anguish of the young virgin turning into a tree to save her honor evoked in all its pain and passion. The cold stone overheated, as it were, bursting forth, as if it had come alive. And yet Penny could only feel the tree growing between her and Michael, the first branches sprouting. She would not stand by passively and let that happen. She was a warrior now, an Amazon. She would fight; her honor demanded no less. Marching back to where Michael stood, looking him dead in the eye, she spoke, determined to make him understand. "You have to talk to me."

"I know. And I will. I promise. But it will be easier for us both if you talk to Artemis first."

Not what she expected to hear. "Artemis? Why?"

"She knows the story and can be objective. We'll see her in a couple of days. Talk to her, and then I'll answer any questions that you have. Trust me. Please."

"What story?"

"Daphne's story."

Penny took a moment, studying the man she loved. He was pleading with her, a hint of desperation in his voice. And he had acknowledged his responsibility to talk to her — that was the important point here. Her worry and concern began to morph into curiosity about Daphne. Curiosity she could live with for a few days. "Ok," she said and smiled. "So... what shall we do now?"

She watched Michael's whole demeanor change, his troubled brow relax, his look one of gratitude and something else, something hotter. "Well," he said seductively, "I can think of a couple of things."

"A couple of things?"

"I'm thinking we might sample some peach gelato at the place we passed, on our way back to the hotel. We might need the extra calories." He grinned.

"Peachy," she replied as she hooked her arm in his.

ΩΩΩ

"Here we are." Michael had pulled the rental car into the parking lot of the Gela Archeological Museum, a short drive from the B&B on the beach where he often stayed when on this errand. They had flown the day before from Florence to Comiso in a tiny twin-engine Piper, with just enough passenger seats for the pair of them and their two Amazon watchers. The Amazons were not happy about the arrangements in Sicily, but Michael had insisted on staying at the B&B Gargone. Their watchers had spent the night in a rented van, taking turns sleeping in the back, where they would find themselves again tonight. The only redeeming feature was the pizzeria down the block.

"The tomb of Aeschylus is in the Museum?" Penny asked, wondering how they would be able to spit on it in there.

"Not inside, right here." He was standing in the adjacent parking space, smirking.

"This is a parking lot, Michael."

"Correct," he smiled. "And two meters down, give or take, are the bones of Aeschylus.

"I thought he had a tomb with a big engraved headstone."

"He did, a little over 2,400 years ago. A lot of history has happened since then. Aeschylus was buried in 456 BC. In 405 BC, Gela was conquered by the Carthaginians, completely destroyed, and left uninhabited for about 70 years." Michael pointed out the excavations to the east. "Over there are what remain of the Gela Acropolis."

"And you're certain his grave is here," Penny said, unable to hide the skepticism in her voice.

"Assuming the Messina earthquake of 1908 didn't move things around too much, absolutely. I made a point of re-marking its location after every invasion, from the southwest corner of the Acropolis wall." Michael hawked and spit, looked up at Penny, smiled. "Care to join me?"

She giggled, cleared her throat, and spit. "Take that, you misogynous, slanderous pig!"

"Well said!" Michael laughed. "The museum actually has some nice Corinthian and Attic vases, if you're interested."

"Well, we're here," she said, smiling, and marched toward the door.

ΩΩΩ

The next morning, after breakfast and a dip in the sea, they packed up their belongings for the 20-mile journey back to the Comiso Airport to meet up with Artemis, Marisol, Helena Zoya, Hermes, and the Gulfstream for the flight back to Boston. Michael dropped her at the private departure lounge with their luggage and drove off to return the car. Once inside, Marisol greeted her with a warm hug. Pulling back, but holding Penny's shoulder, examining her at arm's length, she asked, "So, good honeymoon?"

"The best," answered Penny, smiling.

"You do know we were getting daily reports from the Amazon watchers. Seems you two spent a great deal of time in your hotel rooms."

Penny blushed. "And I imagine you spent all your time milking the goats on Karpathos."

"Touché." Marisol laughed. "I did visit the goats a few times, when Harry went across to pick up supplies."

"Seriously, how's that going?"

"Seriously, is the right word for it. Harry wants to get married, have kids."

"What are you going to do?" Penny asked, concerned for her friend.

"I am going to think about it. Besides, I am an Amazon now, remember? Part of your security detail. So nothing can happen before your baby is born."

Looking around the lounge, Penny asked, "Where are the others?"

"Artemis and Helena are still on board. They are anxious to get underway. I was sent to hurry you along." She smiled.

"Michael's just returning the rental car. He should be here soon."

Right on cue, Michael walked in. "All aboard," Marisol called out.

ΩΩΩ

Once at cruising altitude, Dr. Zoya took Penny aside for a cursory examination and peppered her with questions. Everything was positive; so far, Penny's pregnancy had been an easy one. No morning sickness to speak of, although certain smells could set her off. Coffee for one. Once Michael had figured that out, he took to drinking black tea in the mornings.

"No cravings?" Helena asked.

"Not for food," Penny replied with a wry smile.

Helena laughed. "That's perfectly normal. Could be in part hormonal changes due to your pregnancy. Then again, could just be the way things are. Either way, please feel free to enjoy yourself. What's good for you is good for the baby." Turning her gaze toward Michael, who had lowered his seat back and was happily sawing wood, she asked, "What about your husband?"

Penny smiled. "As you can see, he seems pretty relaxed, about most things." But saying this, she was reminded of Daphne and resolved to talk with Artemis sooner, rather than later. "He's a little overprotective, perhaps, like everyone, *Doctor*, but I really don't mind."

"It is well you don't mind." She smiled. "You are my sister now, not just my patient, and you are much loved and respected by all of us. So, yes, you will be protected, and overly so."

Examination over, Michael sleeping peacefully, Penny slipped into the seat next to Artemis, who immediately began talking hurriedly, as was her way. "I've been looking at the engravings Hephaestus gave you. Reading the ancient Greek is fun for me, and there's some really interesting stuff too."

"Anything about Daphne?" Penny asked.

That stopped her. "As a matter of fact, there is," said Artemis, her brow creased, her eyes speculative. "Why do you ask?" to which Penny recounted the events at the *Bargello*.

Artemis took a deep breath and sighed. "Do you know the story of Persephone?"

"Daughter of Demeter and Zeus, abducted by Hades, pomegranate seeds, the cycle of seasons."

"Yes, well, most of that's a crock. Demeter actually had twin daughters by a mortal who she never named, Persephone and Daphne. No Hades, no abduction, no pomegranate seeds. Daphne was always sickly — probably a victim of childhood leukemia. Even as an infant, my brother was drawn to her, and the feeling was mutual. The good news is you need not worry about Michael being a good father. He was that and more to Daphne.

"Demeter, bless her soul, loved both her daughters, but she didn't know how to deal with Daphne. You have to understand, back then any physical ailment or deformity was treated with disdain, and immortals especially never had to deal with such things. But Michael cared for her, played with her, and when she was older, talked with her, taught her things about the world. He would chase her on the slopes of Mt.

Olympus, not to rape her, for heaven's sake, but to hug her, and tickle her, and make her laugh.

"And she taught him about mortality. She knew she was going to die, and she considered that knowledge a blessing. It meant, she said, that every day was much more special. She was only 12 when she died. He was with her, feeling helpless, no doubt. All he could do was plant a laurel tree by her grave — she loved the scent of laurel. He was depressed for months, years even, grieving. That's probably not something he wanted to relive on your honeymoon."

Penny was quiet, alone with her thoughts. Michael would never forget Daphne, and he shouldn't. It was a beautiful story, albeit with a sad ending, that spoke volumes about his character. But after three millennia, the pain was still raw, and that she felt was unhealthy. She would have to find a way to help him let that go. After a few moments, she turned toward Artemis and thanked her, and they exchanged sad smiles.

"There's something else I've been meaning to ask you," she said. "Everyone seems so concerned about my safety, not that I'm complaining. But just how dangerous is Aphrodite?"

Artemis sighed. "I suppose you have a right to know. Do you know the story of Medea?"

"I know about Jason and the Golden Fleece and Euripides's play."

Artemis nodded. "Ok, now cast Aphrodite as Medea."

"Do you mean she's like Medea?" Penny asked, feeling a frisson of fear, a chill rising up her spine.

"No. I mean she *was* Medea."

Penny gasped. "Oh my God!"

"She and Jason were two of a kind: both manipulative, both self-absorbed, both seeking thrills. They bonded over the theft of the Golden Fleece, and they had a child together. The details vary from the stories you've read, but the particulars aren't really important. Euripides's play comes pretty close to the truth. Jason intended to betray her, supposing that she would believe his claim that marrying the young princess would benefit them both. The princess she poisoned, their son she stabbed to death."

Penny paled as her hand covered her belly.

"Now you know why we're so careful," Artemis continued. "But we are careful. We won't let anything happen to you." She reached over and gently stroked Penny's cheek. "Trust me."

After a couple of slow deep breaths, Penny started to calm. She did trust Artemis and the Amazons. They were careful — careful and competent. She recalled the elaborate ruse they had designed to lure Aphrodite away from Boston. Perhaps they would never have to deal with an immediate threat, but she knew that was unlikely. There would be a confrontation, and she would steel herself for that moment. She would prepare herself mentally to make good decisions. It would be the downhill run of her life, literally, and she would be ready. She was an Amazon now. Her breathing normal, the blood returning to her face, she faced Artemis. "I will do whatever I have to."

Artemis smiled. "I know you will. Now, why don't you get some rest. It's a long flight yet."

Penny slid back into the seat next to her sleeping husband, dropped the seat back, and slept. She awoke, having dreamt again of a young girl with olive skin and auburn hair romping in the surf, only this time she knew where she was: the Sarian beach where she had been married. She turned her head toward Michael, who was watching her with a soft smile on his lips and wonder in his eyes. "Hi," she said. "Are we there yet?"

Michael chuckled. "Couple of hours still. Sleep well?"

"I did." She raised the seat so they were face to face. "Have you given any thought to a name for our daughter?"

"I always thought we would call her Diana."

"I am *not* naming my child after Wonder Woman," Penny snapped.

Michael laughed. "Well, have you a better idea?"

She undid her seat belt, moved closer to him. "I was thinking we could call her Daphne."

She watched the tears form in his eyes, crawled onto his lap, held him tight, tucked against his shoulder, and he cried and cried, as the plane chased the setting sun all the way to Boston.

CHAPTER 9

Friday night dinners had become something of a ritual. Artemis and Cynna would join the residents of the Castle in Cambridge, as Penny had come to call it, and not just to enjoy one of Marisol's fabulous meals — this time, *Asopao de Pollo*, a hearty gumbo-like stew — but to catch up on the week, to review plans and ideas, and to surreptitiously slip tasty morsels to Sappho under the table. This evening, Marisol was reporting what she had heard from Hephaestus, at least the part suitable for public consumption, including Frank's latest design for a drip irrigation system. She faced Penny and smirked. "Your father has a man-crush on my man."

Penny giggled. "You may be right."

"Oh, she's right," chimed in Alice. "When your parents stayed with me, Siobhan and I thought we'd have to twist Frank's arm a bit to get him completely on board. If anything, it was the other way around. That Harry knows what he's about, he told us, time the real criminals get a taste of their own medicine."

"Harry actually appreciates the help," said Marisol. "Frank has good ideas, he says, especially about water systems."

All the while, Michael appeared to be gazing longingly at the half-empty bottle of Malbec, which had not gone unnoticed by Penny. "Go ahead, pour yourself a glass. I don't mind, really."

Michael sat straight up, having been caught as it were with his hand in the cookie jar. "No, we're pregnant. The next wine I have will be shared with you."

"I'll be nursing after the baby is born, you know. Could be years."

His horrified look elicited a round of chuckles. "You're kidding, right?"

"Of course she's kidding," Alice said, picking up the Malbec and refilling her own glass with a wry smile. "How are classes going, Penny?"

"I'm thinking about writing a paper on the Eleusinian Mysteries for my Ancient Cultures Seminar. The standard mythology of Demeter and Persephone, based on the *Homeric Hymns*, as well as the scholarly interpretations of the Mysteries themselves, are incomplete and skewed because they lack an account of Daphne, which I now have, and can document with Harry's engravings. But that's the problem."

"You can't really cite them," said Michael, completing her thought.

"Why not?" asked Marisol, all eyes turning in her direction. "Hephaestus, God of Fire, engraved journal, c. 950 BC." She smiled sweetly at Michael.

"You can't be serious," Michael replied.

"But I am," she said, "and I have already discussed the idea with Hephaestus. He likes it. Think about the excitement the discovery of the engravings would create, and not just among scholars. All that interest focused on the classical world view, the classical vision of the good life, the subject matter of the liberal arts."

"Interesting." And it was, Michael thought. "Five hundred years of notes, written by the same hand, an Olympian god no less, talking about other Olympians. Certain to raise eyebrows. I wonder if it's the kind of attention that would be well received by the elders of Mt. Olympus."

"What harm could it really do?" asked Marisol. "You Olympians have done a masterful job of disguising yourselves and blending in, for thousands of years. Besides, Harry says Athena can convince Zeus of anything."

Artemis chuckled. "He's right about that."

"Of course, the whole thing might shine a bright spotlight on Penny that Aphrodite couldn't fail to see," Michael continued, thinking out loud.

"That might be a good thing," said Penny. "Time is pressing in on Aphrodite, and I don't want harm coming to anyone because of me. I'd much rather confront her directly."

"Spoken like a true Amazon!" beamed Cynna.

Artemis took over now, carefully choosing her words, so Penny would know she was being honest and forthright. "We've got eyes on the Bitch Goddess in Montreal, and we do expect her to make a move soon. But she'll want to confirm the identity of her target before she acts in earnest. Once she discovers she's been duped, as she will likely do, we think she will return to Boston. Now that she is in our sights, however, we can more easily anticipate her plans and thwart them. Spotlight or not, some kind of confrontation with her will probably happen here. Trust me, we will be ready."

"There will be no spotlight," said Marisol. "The University will want to confirm the authenticity of something so incredible before letting word leak out. First, they will analyze the Greek, and will discover it to be Archaic and stylistically consistent, by one hand, as you put it. Then they will want to date the metal. All of that will take time."

"How do you know this?" asked Penny, genuinely curious.

Marisol smiled. "Research."

"Can metal even be dated?" Michael asked.

"According to my man, a process called voltammetry dating can be used, because of the copper in the alloy. A few phone calls to MIT confirmed both that fact, and that they can do the testing there."

"You've given this a lot of thought," said Michael. "Is this what you do when you Skype with Harry? Discuss brilliant ideas?" He smirked.

Marisol blushed a shade probably only apparent to Penny. "We discuss brilliant ideas of all kinds."

ΩΩΩ

A New Look at the Eleusinian Mysteries — Penny's rather pedestrian title for her first seminar paper, given the explosiveness of the content within. Of course, she did not lead with the incendiary material; the bombs were hidden well away, literally in the footnotes. After all, this was a graduate school essay, not a tabloid exposé. Like all graduate school essays, she began with a review of the literature.

The scholarship was in general agreement about a number of points. First, that the root of the Mysteries was agrarian, probably with influences traceable to Mycenaean religious practices and even farther back to the Minoan civilization. The footnote documenting the sources for these claims went further than necessary, offering the first hint of things to come. In it, Penny asserted her belief that the Minoan connection was more significant than previously thought, and that she hoped to more fully develop the relationship between the Minoan and Hellenic civilizations in her dissertation.

Second, the myth of Demeter and Persephone was central, both to the origins of the Mysteries and the rites performed therein, and provided the mythical explanation for the cycle of the seasons. The annual rites denoted as the "Lesser Mysteries" by most scholars were performed around the Spring equinox, corresponding to Persephone's return from Hades, as proclaimed in the Homeric *Hymn to Demeter*. The

"Greater Mysteries," lasting between ten days and two weeks, occurred around the beginning of September. Little is known about the purpose or specific character of the rites performed at either time, leaving much room for conjecture. Penny intended to enter that realm of speculation, but armed with some hitherto unknown facts.

These would be the facts told to her by Artemis and now documented by Harry's plates, that Demeter had twin daughters by an unnamed mortal, one of whom died young. She footnoted the appropriate passages, attributing them to Hephaestus, and showing both the original Greek and the English translation by Michael — which they decided she would claim as her own, with his assistance. And to that note, she appended this: "I am not prepared to argue at this time that the persons named in the engraving are gods, or what that might mean, although I hope to be able to do so as part of my dissertation. I will, however, stand by the authenticity of my source, and assert without qualification that the persons so named are the factual subjects upon which the relevant mythology is predicated."

There was little doubt, Penny argued, that the cult of Demeter and Persephone authored and organized the Eleusinian Mysteries, but what she now knew undercut the prevailing assumption that the myth revolving around the abduction of Persephone by Hades was at their core. The death of Daphne at an early age provided an alternative explanation for Demeter's gloom, as well as strong evidence that her twin sister, Persephone, could not have been the immortal goddess portrayed in the myth. Moreover, the Homeric *Hymn to Demeter* explicitly proclaimed Persephone's "rebirth" in the "bountiful springtime," which did not square with the climate of ancient Greece, where the summer months of drought would have been the time of fallow fields. She maintained, in short, that to properly understand the Mysteries, their agrarian roots must be severed.

The Lesser Mysteries, by all accounts, were largely about purification. Held at the village of Agrae on the banks of the Ilissus River, east of Athens, participants would make sacrifices to Demeter and Persephone, fast, and then ritually purify themselves in the river. Once completed, participants would be deemed *mystai* or initiates, worthy of the Greater Mysteries. Begging the question: purified for what purpose? To which Penny proposed her own answer. Suppose Demeter held herself responsible for the illness that killed Daphne — citing here a supporting passage from Hephaestus's engravings. Perhaps she felt herself to be impure, or the love that resulted in her pregnancy to be such. The *mystai* might not be interested in agricultural production, but in their own reproduction. The Lesser Mysteries to purify themselves for the planting of seeds during the period of the Greater Mysteries — making the latter something like a couples' retreat — with the birth of healthy children in the "bountiful springtime," as promised to Persephone.

Finally, while beyond the scope of her central thesis, Penny felt compelled to note that the death of Daphne at age 12 put the lie to the myth of Apollo and Daphne, propagated most prominently by Ovid. There was evidence, again citing Hephaestus, that Apollo knew Daphne, and even held strong feelings of love for her. But not erotic love (*eros*), rather *agapê* (charity) and *philos* (friendship). The laurel wreath Apollo is often depicted wearing was thought to be a symbol of his eternal love for Daphne, and was in fact awarded to the victors of the Pythian or Delphic Games held in his honor; however, not because Daphne was turned into a laurel tree to avoid her rape, but because Apollo planted a laurel tree at her gravesite to show his enduring and deep affection for her.

Whatever the merits of her interpretation, Penny knew it would be the skepticism surrounding her primary source that would raise concerns. So she was not surprised to receive an email from Professor

THE OAR OF ODYSSEUS   **175**

Jensen, inviting her to his office to discuss her paper. She and Michael had worked out a plausible story regarding the provenance of the engravings, which they shared with Artemis and Marisol, and rehearsed as many interview scenarios as they could anticipate. Penny felt well prepared and confident as she strolled to Dr. Jensen's office, Sappho trotting at her side.

Jensen was a little taken aback at the sight of the dog, but smiled when Penny said, "I thought I might need a witness." His smile turned into a chuckle when she added, "This is Sappho, and she's not growling — that has to be a good sign." He was a dog person, she knew, from remarks he'd made in class. Penny took the proffered chair, settling Sappho at her feet, and handed Jensen a manila folder.

"What's this?" he asked, opening the folder and laying out its contents.

"Photographs of what we're here to discuss. You can understand why I wouldn't want to carry them around with me. They could be worth a small fortune."

"If they're authentic," he said.

"I believe they are, but I'm anxious to have that established independently. I'm hoping to have a discussion with someone here who can make that happen. I could go to an auction house, or a private collector, but I would much prefer to have the engravings remain available for academic research, starting with my own." She smiled.

"If they are genuine, antiquities law might require their return to Greece."

"Way ahead of you there. I've retained a lawyer, who assures me that given the manner in which I acquired them, antiquities law would not apply. They were a gift to me, from a man whose family had held them privately for generations. I would be happy to share that story with you, as it speaks to my belief in their authenticity."

"Please."

"We were in Gela, Sicily, my husband and I, in the parking lot of the Archeological Museum, when this very old but spry gentleman walked up and told us we were standing on Aeschylus's grave. We looked puzzled, so he explained. Pointing to the ruins of the Gela Acropolis, adjacent to the Museum, he said as a child he had studied an old map of the ancient Greek town, and the tomb of Aeschylus was well marked, maybe ten meters outside the Acropolis wall. None of it remained then, of course, but once the ruins had been excavated, his father brought him here, and the two of them figured out where the tomb had to have been — right where we were standing.

"He told us his family had long roots in Gela, dating back to ancient times. He knew all kinds of history about the place, and once he found out I was a classics student, he insisted on showing us around the ruins and the Museum. He told us folks called him Gyftos — that word mean anything to you?" she asked, wrote it out in Greek (γύφτος) and showed it to him. Jensen shook his head.

"It means gypsy in contemporary Greek, but an older meaning is blacksmith." She let that sink in for a moment, and then continued. "In any event, he asked us to meet him for dinner that evening; he had something he wanted to give me. So we met him at *Trattoria San Giovanni*, and he gave me the box you see there in the photos, filled with 48 engraved plates, numbered with the Greek alphabet, in two series. As far as I have been able to determine, it covers about 500 years, roughly from 1100 to 700 BC, one plate every decade or so. He said the plates had been in his family forever, but there was no one left to leave them to — he was the last of his line. Why not leave them to the Museum, I asked. He didn't trust government institutions, he said, all corrupt. Wanted me to have them, said he trusted me. Besides, he said, it had to be Fate that brought us together at the grave of Aeschylus.

"We left the next day on a private jet leased to my husband's security company. There were others on the plane to whom we told this story. My lawyer called it contemporaneous testimony — enough to prevail in any challenge to my claim in the absence of adverse evidence."

Jensen was quiet, clearly trying to assess the veracity of what he had just heard. Finally, he spoke. "You want the University to date and authenticate the engravings?"

"Yes. I'm willing to enter into some kind of agreement to make that happen. Ultimately, I would like to transfer the whole box to the University, with a set of conditions to guarantee access for research rather than commercial purposes."

"Why would you do that?" he asked, incredulous.

"You mean, why not sell to the highest bidder and retire?" She smiled. "I think Gyftos picked me for a reason. You surely understand that people don't study the classics to become rich. Right now, the question is when and if you can arrange to have the plates tested."

"Let me make some calls and get back to you. Are the plates secured?"

Penny smiled once more. "As I said, my husband owns a security firm. Anything else?"

"The translations are quite good. You say they're yours?"

"Yes, but I had a lot of help."

"Oh?'

"From a few folks you know well: Liddell and Scott, and Herbert Weir Smyth," she said, nodding toward the *Greek-English Lexicon* and the *Greek Grammar* on the bookshelf to her right. "And my husband," she added, "who is Greek by birth."

ΩΩΩ

The wind had come up, the cold seeping through the seams of Penny's quilted down jacket. Fortunately, the coffee shop was only a couple blocks from the seminar room where her class had just ended, and even at seven months pregnant, she could still walk at a pace to keep her blood pumping and her extremities warm. The text message said to meet at the coffee shop at 3:30; she would be a few minutes early. Σαρια was scarcely populated this time of day, but warm and inviting, as was the smile on Cynna's face behind the counter.

"Hey you," Cynna greeted her brightly. "What's happening?"

"Got a message to meet Artemis here," Penny replied, as she pushed back the hood of her coat and unzipped it. Looking up at the now-familiar photograph of Saria, she sighed, wistfully longing for the sunnier clime.

"Haven't seen her. Can I get you something?"

"I think I'm early. Ginger tea, maybe a bagel, with cream cheese."

Cynna smiled. "Sure thing. I'll bring it to the corner booth."

Penny barely had time to shed her coat and settle in before Cynna arrived with a steaming pot and a toasted blueberry bagel. "That was quick," she said and added with a smirk, "Seems like you've been spending a lot of time at the Cambridge Castle of late."

"Maybe," said the pretty Amazon, blushing.

"So things are serious?"

"Serious is too strong a word. But things are real." Cynna took a seat. "At first it was just fun, you know, casual, something different for both of us. But Alice is a remarkable woman."

Penny smiled. "That she is. I'm happy for both of you."

"It does seem like everyone close to you is falling in love." Cynna's turn to smirk.

"You can't blame this on me," protested Penny.

"I wouldn't think of it. You're my sister, and I would never accuse you of anything, except maybe being pregnant."

Penny giggled. "It is getting harder to reach the table."

Both their heads turned toward the front of the shop when the door opened and noisily admitted Artemis with Sappho in tow — at least for the moment. Sappho spotted Penny first and proceeded to drag Artemis to the booth in back. Cynna stood, surrendering her place to Artemis, as Penny cupped Sappho's head in her hands with obvious affection and asked, "What are you doing here?"

"I stopped at the house to talk with Alice and Marisol, and Sappho insisted on coming," Artemis explained.

Penny giggled as she scratched Sappho's ears. "Leash in her mouth, blocking the door?"

"Exactly." She turned to Cynna. "Could you bring me an Americano and then keep watch?"

Cynna's demeanor changed immediately. All business now, and not the business of a barista.

"What's wrong?" Penny asked.

Artemis sighed. "Probably nothing to be concerned about at the moment. Aphrodite is on the move, heading this way. She is quite adept at recruiting unwitting confederates, so everyone is on high alert. We have no idea if she has anyone in place here."

"What happened?" Penny protectively rubbed her belly, and Sappho emitted a low growl.

"A very well planned electrical fire. Actually, more smoke than fire, enough to literally smoke out our decoys in the middle of the night. No doubt so she could get a look at them out of character — our Jennifer not pregnant, our Sara not a man. Maybe she seduced the meter reader; we're not sure. But no one was hurt, and we've still got eyes on her."

"What now?"

"We wait. We watch. We need to determine what she knows and what she's planning. We've already prepared a few scenarios for taking her down, which can be adjusted once we know more. Zeus and Ares are on their way here. They'll stay close. If we catch her clearly violating the order of the Olympian Council, Zeus will have no choice but to punish her."

"Punish her?"

Artemis laughed, shaking her head ruefully. "Zeus will lock her in her room on Mt. Olympus, and Ares will make sure she stays put. In any event, we think Saria may be the safest place for you to give birth. One way or another, we'll get you there as soon as the semester ends."

Penny sighed. "At least it will be warm."

ΩΩΩ

Professor Carl Whitmore opened the email marked urgent from Graduate Dean, Susan Brinkley, with a growing sense of foreboding. "Please make time to meet with me and Ms. Penelope Bauer, this afternoon, at 4 p.m." She knew his schedule; she knew he had to be on campus and available at that hour.

So what? The little tramp in his Homer Seminar had apparently gone to the Dean because he'd flunked her. What was he supposed to do? Citing the Greek God of Fire, or at least someone named Hephaestus, from an unpublished and apparently unknown engraved journal. Making outrageous claims about the Trojan War, Achilles, and Homer himself. He pulled up the paper on his computer to refresh his memory, so he'd have his facts down pat.

Ms. Bauer claimed that Helen was really Aphrodite, the Goddess of Love, who married Hephaestus on a lark, and dumped him almost immediately for Menelaus. She then ran off with Paris, intending to start a war to stroke her warped sense of self. Nothing like hundreds of men fighting and dying over her. All of this was documented from the unpublished journal of Hephaestus, supplemented by some cited works in abnormal psychology regarding narcissistic personality disorder. Poppycock! According to Ms. Bauer, finally citing some legitimate sources, the Trojan War was not in the end about Helen, aka Aphrodite, but about Achaean greed. Here, Whitmore had to admit, she made a fairly compelling argument.

However, she then went on to make the outlandish assertion that Achilles never fought and died in Troy, and was not even alive during that time period. Rather, he was nothing more than a ripped bartender in some ancient Mycenaean saloon who caught the eye of Homer, a young and talented rhapsode. The Achilles of the *Iliad* was Homer's creation, she argued, first sung about in that seedy establishment in his effort to seduce the real Achilles. Such slander! Again, she relied almost entirely on the testimony of Hephaestus to support these claims, coupled with some interesting analysis of the Greek Homer used when describing Achilles in the *Iliad* — irrelevant unless one accepted her initial contention. Whitmore could barely contain his fury.

On the other hand, Penny could barely contain her glee. Dr. Brinkley, the Graduate Dean, who had overseen the University's efforts to authenticate and date the engravings, had provided her with a copy of the final report yesterday, confirming what Penny already knew. She would be meeting with the Dean this afternoon, first to deal with Professor Whitmore — who was known among her fellow students as Professor Witless — and then to discuss the terms of the possible transfer of the plates to the University. Whitmore's reaction to her seminar paper had been expected, but the vehemence with which he had promised to see her booted from the Classics Department, bordering on the pathological, had made her chuckle. She would let the Dean deal with him. As for the negotiations regarding the plates, she was comfortable with the proposal drafted over a Friday dinner at the Cambridge Castle and refined by Abigail Fowler, Alice's lawyer and former lover.

Penny arrived at the Dean's office a few minutes early and was immediately admitted. They shook hands and Penny took a seat. "I trust you got the copy of Professor Whitmore's comments to my paper. I was hoping that you would take the lead with him," she said.

"Yes. I think that wise," the Dean replied, taking her place behind her rather imposing desk.

"There won't be any issues with Professor Jensen. I gave him a copy of the report earlier today. He seemed quite pleased."

"As he should be. What a fascinating discovery." The intercom buzzed, the Dean's assistant announcing the arrival of Professor Whitmore. "Send him in." She smiled at Penny, reassuringly, and rose to greet Whitmore. "Dr. Whitmore, please have a seat. You know Ms. Bauer, of course."

"I do," he grumbled, sitting in the chair next to Penny's, uncomfortably, or so it seemed.

Before returning to her own chair, the Dean reached across her desk to offer him a copy of the authentication results. "You must have assumed that I called you here to discuss your assessment of Ms. Bauer's work." He nodded, glancing down at the document in his hand, and she continued. "The report you have there speaks to the authentication of the engravings that Ms. Bauer cites in her paper. I caution you that we are revealing these details on a need-to-know basis only. You will note that the University's most accomplished Greek scholars have concluded that the Greek itself is Archaic and more likely than not the work of a single individual. Also, according to the tests performed by MIT metallurgical scientists, the metal plates are roughly 3,000 years old, or more precisely, dating from about 1100 BC to 700 BC. To be blunt, Ms. Bauer is citing testimony contemporary to the events she describes in her paper — a legitimate use of documentation by any academic standard I am aware of."

"But she claims Achilles was a bartender!" Whitmore roared.

"With acceptable documentation," the Dean calmly replied. "And you must admit, her translations are above reproach."

"Excuse me," injected Penny. "For the record, my husband helped me with the translations."

"So noted," said Dr. Brinkley.

"I have studied Homer my whole adult life! You can't really believe the musings of this little tart over me," he shrieked.

"Professor Witless," shouted the Dean, then recovered herself. "Professor Whitmore, I suggest you apologize to Ms. Bauer immediately. Your language constitutes sexual harassment of an actionable nature." Whitmore remained silent, fuming. The Dean rose from her seat, leaned forward, placing her palms flat on her desk, and addressed him as if he'd been called to the principal's office. "Then listen very carefully to me. You will reassess Ms. Bauer's work, and if I see that it receives anything less than the "A" it deserves, you will find yourself defending your actions and your words before Academic Standards and the Judicial Board. Do I make myself clear?"

"Are you threatening me?" he challenged.

"Of course, I am. Which part did you not understand?" She sat back down. "You may leave now."

Whitmore, grumbling to himself, left the office in a huff. Penny sat in stunned silence.

Dr. Brinkley took a deep breath. "Well, that's dealt with." She smiled. "Please don't fret. Drama is all part of the academic life, as is misogyny, unfortunately." Then, as if nothing had happened, "So, you wanted to discuss your ideas for transferring the plates to the University."

"I did. I mean, I do. Yes." Penny reached into her backpack, pulled out a folder, and handed a sheet of paper with Abigail Fowler's letterhead to the Dean. "These are the ideas I've discussed with my lawyer. First, money. My family wants to start a foundation devoted to the advancement of the liberal arts. The University would contribute one million dollars to that foundation, and two percent of any profits it receives from the sale of items connected to the engravings, such as translations and photo images. In addition, my friend Marisol Rivera and I would be allowed to take graduate courses at the University free of tuition and fees. This is not a guarantee of any sort of degree, just access to courses."

"Who is this Marisol, if I may ask?"

Penny smiled. "She is a refugee from Hurricane Maria in Puerto Rico, which took everything she had. She has a BS in environmental science, but has become fascinated by the classics. She is at least as intelligent and capable as I am, if not more so. She is my dearest friend and confidant. And she deserves a break."

The Dean nodded. "I see."

"Ok. Second, the University would be barred from selling the engravings to any private collector, but only to another academic institution which, like the University, will be required to make the engravings available for bona fide academic research, with reasonable safeguards regarding actual access. Third, and most important to me, I want to hold on to the entire collection until the summer. I'm going to take a leave of absence, to care for my newborn, but also to finish my translation and write an article anticipating my dissertation, to protect my claim to original research."

"I'm guessing you already know what you want to write."

"I do. I want to make the case that Hephaestus, the god, is the actual author, and even the man who gifted the engravings to me. And that the references to other gods and goddesses by name are genuine."

"So you think the Olympian gods are real, or were real?"

"Yes. In fact, I think all civilizations have gods of this sort — not all-knowing or all-powerful, but carriers of the civilization's values. And I believe such gods live and die with the civilizations they embody." She paused. "The man who gave me the plates said he was the last of his line. I think he was the last of the Olympians. The rest of the Greek gods had already faded away, as what they recognized as Western civilization was rotting from within."

CHAPTER 10

Another Friday night dinner at the Cambridge Castle, this time with Marisol's version of *pernil*, pulled pork with *mojo* sauce, served with black beans and Spanish rice. Alice waited until everyone had eaten their fill, more or less, before announcing her news of the day. "I got a call from Abi Fowler this morning," she said.

Artemis chuckled. "Ms. Fowler wants to introduce you to a new financial planner in town, a Sirena Johnson, who has creative investment ideas, and who is even more creative in the bedroom."

"Abi only hinted at the latter, but yes. So I was right to be suspicious."

"Indeed," said Artemis. "Sirena Johnson is the newest incarnation of Aphrodite. Google the name and at first blush she looks impressive, but her cover story is only one layer thick. The Forbes profile, for example, is fake, as are all her degrees and certificates. Her web page and Facebook page are barely two weeks old. The only thing true about Sirena is her talent in bed."

"So, I let her lure me to bed and press a pillow over her face?" Alice smirked.

"Actually," said Artemis, "we have something very much like that in mind."

"You want me to sleep with her?" Alice asked, horrified.

"You might learn something," whispered a blushing Cynna to a blushing Alice. Clearly a reference to some private joke, arousing the curiosity of everyone at the table, none of whom were brave enough to pursue it.

Artemis laughed. "No, not sleep with her. Aphrodite can read emotions, remember? It's important that she not know that you are on to her. Penny, when are you finished?"

"I have classes on Monday and Wednesday, but I've already done my presentations, so I could miss either. The deal with the University is done; I just need to sign the papers."

"Let's plan on Thursday," said Artemis after a moment of thought. "Penny, you and Michael will fly out then. Alice, tell Abi you could have dinner with her and Sirena one evening early in the week. We'll talk more about how that should go, but you will invite Sirena to come here on Thursday evening, presumably for an erotic encounter. There are details to work out, but that's when we will take her down."

"So Aphrodite knows it's me," Penny said to Artemis, annoyed.

"We believe she does."

"Why didn't you tell me?"

"You're safe, trust me. Security around you has never been tighter. But the more normal everything looks, the better our chances of trapping her. If, for example, you were constantly looking over your shoulder, it might tip her off that we know she's here and watching you. That's why I didn't tell you. A strategic decision. Now we know how she's planning to get close, so now's the time to act."

Penny listened, considered, and was mostly mollified. She knew that Artemis had her best interest at heart — as did all the Amazons. "Ok. But you know I hate being kept in the dark."

THE OAR OF ODYSSEUS

"I do. Michael has told me." She said, a knowing glance at her brother, immediately lightening the mood.

Penny narrowed her eyes at Michael. "I'll deal with you later."

"I'm looking forward to it." He smiled.

Marisol took the opportunity to change the subject. "I am grateful that you included me in your deal with the University, Penny."

Penny shook her head, smiling. "I should be thanking you — we all should. We both know that if not for you there would be no deal. In fact, more than likely, the engravings would still be collecting dust in Saria."

"Nevertheless. I have been blessed and feel nothing but gratitude."

"Me too," said Penny. "I just wish it weren't so damn cold."

ΩΩΩ

Michael climbed into bed later that evening, snuggled up to his very pregnant wife, lying peacefully on her back, and kissed her softly on the lips. "Are you scared?" he asked.

"Not scared. Anxious, maybe." She sighed. "To be gone from here. To finally meet our Daphne." She took his hand and placed it on her belly.

"She's kicking," he said, wonder in his voice.

"Dancing." Penny smiled at the love of her life. "When I'm moving around, she sleeps. When I'm ready to sleep, she dances. Helena says that's normal. I'm telling you right now, that will have to change after she's born."

Michael laughed. "I'll see to it, dear."

"How are things going in the Bunker?"

"All the equipment is in place. Arina is in charge of all that now, running tests. Hephaestus tells me they've taken to calling her Cyborg because she's living inside the servers and the code. But he expects things to be ready to go live by mid-January, about the time our little one is due." Michael kissed her again. "I'm really proud of you, you know. One semester and you've already made a name for yourself."

"Maybe so. But a lot of that has to do with the engravings."

"Sometimes I worry that I've passed onto you some of my worst habits. Gyftos. The ability to lie convincingly."

"A noble lie, to quote some loquacious philosopher. More accurately, the truth, just dressed up in disguise. After all, they were a gift from Hephaestus. And even though you did the translations for my papers, I've learned a lot of ancient Greek. Enough to lie convincingly." She smiled sweetly.

"All of you O'Connor women have smart mouths."

"It does run in the family." She pushed herself up, with some difficulty, and rolled Michael on his back. "Let me show how smart mine is."

ΩΩΩ

Tuesday night, at almost 11 p.m., Sappho leaped from the sofa, where she had been comfortably settled between Michael and Penny, and the recipient of much affection from both of them. She pranced happily at the front door, whimpering as dogs do. Alice opened the door and greeted Sappho with a big smile, finally back from her dinner with Abi Fowler and Sirena, aka Aphrodite. The smile was still plastered on her face when she entered the living room, and with a sweeping flourish of her arm, worthy of a trashy Hollywood movie, she said, "Good evening!"

"A little tipsy, are you?" Penny inquired, suppressing a giggle.

"I may have had a martini or three — enough to hide my true feelings," she said, plopping into an overstuffed chair.

"You appear to be feeling just fine, *Tía*," Penny said, no longer able to contain her giggle.

"That I am, dear heart."

Marisol had quietly slipped into the kitchen, returning with a steaming mug of black coffee. "Thank you, dear," said Alice, taking a sip.

"Did you sleep with her?" asked Cynna.

"With who?" Alice screwed up her face. "Or would it be whom?"

"Oh God," mumbled Artemis, under her breath.

Cynna pressed on. "With Sirena, Aphrodite, you know, the Bitch Goddess."

"Of course not. Told her I'm not much for strange hotel rooms. So I invited her to come here on Thursday."

"What time?" asked Artemis.

"Oh, it must be after 11, don't you think?"

"No, Alice," said an increasingly exasperated Artemis. "What time is she coming here on Thursday?"

"As we discussed. She's to come at 7 for a light dinner and... whatever." Alice smiled, drinking more coffee and trying at least to recover a semblance of her wits.

"And the other things we discussed? Can you recall what else was said?"

"Abi asked about Penny, so everything came out naturally. How Penny lives in the apartment downstairs with Michael. How very pregnant she is. How she is a graduate student at BU."

Artemis was nodding, ticking off each point. "Excellent. Anything else?"

"There was a lot of flirting. I told her I was quite happy with my financial position, and that she'd have to be spectacular in bed if she were going to get an opportunity to play with my money. She laughed at that. Abi said Sirena could be quite persuasive, then suggested the possibility of a threesome." Alice giggled.

"Any indication that Sirena was at all suspicious?"

"None."

"Well done, Alice," said Artemis, who then turned to Marisol. "Maybe a round of coffee for everyone before I lay out the plan for Thursday."

After everyone had a little coffee, and Alice a little more, Artemis described the plan and issued assignments. She was convinced that Aphrodite had secured the services of a private detective agency, probably with a combination of sex and money, which meant the Cambridge house was under surveillance, Penny and possibly Michael were being shadowed, and the house phone lines were probably tapped. All this could be used to their advantage so long as everything appeared to be happening for real. "The play's the thing," she said, "wherein we catch the conscience of the king."

ΩΩΩ

At about 5 p.m. on Thursday, Marisol left the house with Sappho on a leash and a small pack on her back. She crossed the highway on the pedestrian bridge to Magazine Beach, deserted at that hour, and let the dog do her business, while she assured herself that no one had followed. Rather than returning to the house, she slipped into a large rented SUV parked in the Morris School lot and drove into Boston, parking in the vicinity of Massachusetts General Hospital.

Sappho would have been a liability when Aphrodite arrived, growling even at the mention of her name. She was not particularly happy about another long plane ride to Karpathos, when Penny told her she would be going back to Saria, but her tail started wagging at least a little when reminded that her friend Selene would be waiting for her there. And a little more when she learned that Penny, Michael, and Marisol would be with her on the plane. Marisol's backpack contained what she would need for a few days until Artemis arrived with the rest of her luggage, as well as the trunk Penny and Michael had packed.

On the landline, Michael called Helena Zoya's cell in a panic, at approximately 5:45, reporting Penny's discomfort from what he believed to be labor. Dr. Zoya, conveniently, was already at Mass General. She would check Penny into a room and meet them at the main Obstetrics desk as soon as they arrived. Michael then presumably texted for an Uber because a car appeared about 10 minutes later at the front of the Cambridge house, driven in fact by an Amazon. Michael, still somewhat in a panic and carrying a small suitcase, helped Penny into the back and joined her there. That car too headed for Mass General, literally just a few minutes away. They met Dr. Zoya, as arranged, and after completing a little paperwork, Helena escorted them down the hall and around the corner to her room— but they kept going, down the stairs and out a side entrance, just as Marisol pulled up to the curb in the SUV. All of them then drove to the private terminal at Logan International, where Hermes was waiting with the Gulfstream. They were airborne, bound for Karpathos, shortly after 7 p.m.

Meanwhile, Sirena had knocked on the door of the Cambridge house at precisely 7 o'clock and had been admitted by Cynna, serving that evening in the role of maid. Her real job was to protect Alice if that became necessary. Cynna had wanted to wear a sexy French maid outfit, but Artemis had nixed that idea.

Sirena was stunning — tall and svelte in three-inch heels. Cynna helped her remove her stylish camel hair coat to reveal a full-length gray wraparound skirt in wool and a cream-colored sleeveless cashmere sweater vest. The skirt did not wrap all the way around, leaving a tasteful slit up the middle, so that the skirt would fall from just above the knee if she crossed her legs. Needless to say, she had a body to die for, and her bare arms and shoulders left Cynna breathless. Sirena's face had a mature look. After all, she was supposed to be in her early forties. A few lines gave her forehead character, but there were no signs of anything that could be called a wrinkle. She had steely blue eyes under perfectly threaded brows, a tiny upturned nose, full lips in an oval face, flat ears sporting elegant hoop earrings, and waves of light brown hair tumbling midway to her waist.

"Oh my," said Alice, her eyes traveling from floor to face, "don't you look delicious." Alice had chosen a New Mexican look. Flared gray wool slacks over cowboy boots, a simple white blouse, and a turquoise and silver belt with matching earrings. "I have red wine open, unless you'd prefer something stronger."

"Wine sounds perfect." Sirena smiled.

"Cynna, dear, two glasses of the Shiraz. We'll sit for a while in the front room."

Sirena wasted no time gathering intelligence, taking her cue from Alice's attire. "Your niece is from New Mexico, if I recall. Did she inspire your outfit?"

"Actually, Penny did bring me the turquoise. I'd love to introduce you, but there was a small emergency." Alice smiled as she led Sirena to the two facing armchairs in the living room, just as Cynna appeared with two glasses of wine. "Cheers," said Alice, raising her glass and taking a sip, as did her guest.

"I hope it's nothing serious," said Sirena.

"Probably not. Michael, her husband, is such a worrywart. He thinks she's gone into labor. So off they went to Mass General." Alice took another sip of wine, watching the hint of panic surface on Sirena's face.

"Really? Will you excuse me for a moment? My phone is vibrating, and I am expecting an important call."

"Of course. Take it in the hallway if you'd like some privacy."

Sirena was already up, pulling her phone from a deep pocket in her skirt, and heading out of the room. "Thank you," she managed to say.

Once clear of the living room, she hit speed dial. "It's me. What have you seen?" She listened to the account; it was just as Alice said. Of course, she hadn't told her minions the whole story, so they had no idea what a trip to Mass General meant. The only thing she could do was go there herself. She hurried back into the front room. "I'm so sorry, but my own emergency has come up. I'm afraid I'll have to take a raincheck."

"That's too bad," said Alice. "Is there anything I can do?"

"No. Thank you, but I really must be on my way." Cynna had already retrieved her coat, which Sirena grabbed on the way out the door.

Cynna ambled back into the living room, a big smile on her face. "Be a shame to let the dinner and the wine go to waste."

Alice returned the smile and raised her glass. "I totally agree."

ΩΩΩ

Sirena pulled to the curb at the front entrance to Mass General, hopped out of her car, and hustled toward the automatic glass doors. "Hey, you can't park there!" someone shouted, only to be ignored. At the information kiosk, she asked for Obstetrics and was told one floor up. She took the stairs.

"Penelope Bauer," she announced at the registration desk. "I'm her aunt, Alice O'Connor. I understand she was admitted earlier today."

"Let me check," the clerk behind the computer screen said, tapping his keyboard with practiced efficiency, but trying Sirena's patience nevertheless. "Yes. She's in room 233, around the corner there."

"Thank you," Sirena said, thinking that if Penny was in a room, she likely had not yet given birth. She moved down the hall with purpose now, steeling herself for the task ahead. She took a deep breath to calm herself as she pulled the door open and slipped inside. The room was dark, the shape of a body just visible in the bed. Suddenly the lights came on, she blinked at their brightness, the shape in the bed had risen up, and she found herself looking into the dark eyes of Ares, fixed in a cold stare, and dressed as a security guard.

"Hello, Sis," he said, not in a friendly way.

But from behind her came an even more chilling voice. "What are you doing here, Aphrodite?"

She turned to confront Zeus. "Daddy!" she cried with faux enthusiasm. He looked the part of a resident psychiatrist— well-styled hair, graying at the temples, glasses rimmed in thick black plastic, his worsted wool suit rumpled, with a tie loosened at the neck. "You know it's just a lark, a little game. I wasn't really going to do anything."

Zeus sighed, his brow furrowed, the look in his dark eyes both sad and ominous. "I've been too easy on you all these many centuries, too forgiving. For goodness sake, I've let you get away with murder, which I have no doubt was your intention here. But no more. My conscience can no longer abide such malevolence."

"I've always made it up to you. You know I can," she pleaded. "I know exactly what you like," she added with a menacing edge.

Zeus chuckled ruefully. "I'm finished with all that. And it's no secret what we've done, so there's no leverage to be had."

"Am I then to be held hostage on Mt. Olympus? Bored out of my skull?"

"For the indefinite future, yes. Perhaps we can find you some help to mend your ways."

"Oh, pooh!" she said.

ΩΩΩ

Daphne Bauer Kalomoira was born at 8:27, Wednesday evening, January 16, 2019, after 16 hours of labor. There were no complications, unless one were to count the broken pinkie Michael suffered when Penny squeezed his hand a little too hard during one particularly brutal contraction. Helena Zoya had overseen the delivery and pronounced mother and baby to be healthy and strong. They were both still asleep the next morning as Michael strolled down to the cove to meet Penny's parents and aunt, who had missed the birth because of a nasty nor'easter that had shut down air traffic out of Logan for two full days.

The greetings were warm and familiar all around. Michael could not wipe the grin from his face as they walked up the hill to the compound. " I don't know what I texted, or even if it got through, so here are all the vitals. Mother and baby are doing fine, sleeping right now. Daphne Bauer Kalomoira, 8 pounds, 9 ounces, 17 inches, blue eyes for the moment, a little bit of hair — five hairs, five shades of auburn."

"What about the delivery? asked Siobhan.

"No complications, but 16 long hours of labor. APGAR of 9. Helena says she only gives a 10 if the baby can recite the alphabet."

"Tearing, drugs?" Siobhan persisted.

"No tearing, no drugs, at least for Penny. Your daughter is as strong as an ox. They gave me a shot for this," he said, holding up his hand, a splint on the pinkie and tape around it and its neighbor.

"Broken finger?" Frank asked.

"Penny's vise grip."

"When can we see them? Don't want to disturb their sleep," said Alice.

"I'm betting they're awake. I'll sneak a look and let you know."

They were awake when he slipped into their room. Penny, sitting with her back against the headboard, tired, bedraggled, with Daphne at her breast — she had never looked so beautiful, Michael thought.

Penny looked up and smiled. "My milk's come in. She's nursing."

Michael carefully joined her on the bed, kissed her cheek. "How does it feel?"

"A little strange, but wonderful." She beamed.

"Your parents and Alice are here."

"She's almost done, I'm sure, and she'll be sleepy. Burp her, wrap her in a blanket, maybe put her in her basket. Either way, you can take her outside to meet them while I take a quick shower."

"Of course. Take your time. They'll be here for a couple weeks, now that they've finally made it."

Michael took Daphne from his wife, placed her over his shoulder, and patted her back gently but firmly until she burped. She was almost asleep, so he swaddled her and placed her in her basket, as he heard the sounds of Penny in the shower. His love for this tiny baby was more than he could have ever imagined. Just looking down at her, sleeping, brought tears to his eyes. Wiping them away, he picked up the basket and took his daughter to meet her American elders.

ΩΩΩ

Michael arranged to have a smaller dinner party in the Royal Pod courtyard, away from the main gathering, to include Penny's family, Artemis, Hephaestus, and Marisol, although he insisted that they all walk to the central courtyard in time for dessert. Alice had smuggled two bottles of Malbec onto the Island, cleared the celebratory consumption of them with Themis, and had sought and received assurances from Dr. Zoya that no harm would come to Daphne if Penny were to have one small glass of wine. Of course, there were no wine glasses to be had, but no one seemed to mind.

Penny was asked to propose a toast. She looked at Michael with a sly smile, both of them surely recalling her toast nine months earlier that had led to all this. But then she raised her glass and her voice, "To family, friends, and fortune." Sappho barked her approval, and everyone drank a reverent sip before digging into the *moussaka*, catered from the central kitchen.

Conversation between bites was free and easy. Artemis recounted the tale of Aphrodite's capture for Penny's parents, praising the acting talents of all involved, but especially Alice, who had the starring role. Hephaestus thanked Frank for his advice on drip systems; they were actually in the process of installing one for the orchards right now. Siobhan apologized to Penny once again for missing the birth. Penny smiled at her mother and kissed her cheek. "It's more than enough that you were present at *my* birth." That drew a laugh from everyone. And Penny took that opportunity to surreptitiously pour the rest of her wine into Michael's empty tumbler, much to his delight.

Marisol announced that she had decided to stay on in Saria, at least until the summer, to no one's surprise. But Alice assured her that she would always have a place to stay when and if she decided to take classes at BU, and that she would be welcome to bring a friend. "Don't be concerned that Cynna is moving in," said added. "She won't be staying in your room."

"I'm shocked," said Siobhan. "Honestly, Alice, isn't that girl a little old for you? I mean, she's like 3,000 years old?"

That too drew a laugh, after which Michael stood and said, "Time for dessert."

Michael carried Daphne in her basket. She'd already had her dinner and slept peacefully through theirs. When they reached the central compound, everyone stood. They had wanted to applaud, but Michael had asked them not to, for the baby's sake. It was immediately clear that the tables had been rearranged, creating a corridor to the center of the courtyard, where stood a newly-planted tree.

"What's this?" asked Penny.

"A laurel tree. Daphne's tree. A gift from Athena," Michael said. "I hope you don't mind, I buried the placenta there. The Navajos, from your neck of the woods, believe burying the placenta roots a child to the earth. I thought we might root Daphne to her birthplace, to Saria, for she will always have roots here, wherever she may find herself."

Perhaps it was hearing her name. Perhaps it was the energy of the place, the Amazons welcoming their new Queen. Perhaps it was nothing like that, but Daphne awoke and gurgled happily. Penny lifted her from the basket, and with Michael by her side, carried the child forward to the margin of soft earth surrounding the laurel. Someone clapped, and then someone else, and soon the courtyard was filled with applause, no doubt for Daphne's sake.

ΩΩΩ

Saturday, January 19, 2019. The atmosphere in the Bunker was charged, abuzz with the heat of the impressive row of servers, the weapons of cyber warfare, tempered by ever-circulating water-cooled air. Penny's skin tingled with the hot and cold, as if rubbed with Chinese liniment. Arina and her cyber warriors stood at the ready to launch the first attack, or rather sat before their computer screens, prepared for any contingency. Athena had flown in that morning with Ares and Hermes to bear witness along with their fellow Olympians, Hephaestus, Artemis, and Michael, as well as Themis, Regent of the Amazons, Penny and her father, Frank, and Marisol. Siobhan and Alice had stayed above ground with Sappho to care for Daphne.

Athena, as always, took command. "Penny, why don't you do the honors," she said.

"Thank you, no," Penny replied. "There are many in the room more deserving than me. Michael and Artemis — this has been their dream for over 20 years. My choice would be the two of them."

"You do it, Michael," prompted Artemis. "You made the big sacrifice."

"That's where you're wrong. I have gained far more than I've given up," he said, pulling Penny close.

"Alright then," said Athena. "It does seem right and proper that the Huntress should let fly the first arrow."

Artemis looked around the room to approving nods from Hephaestus and Themis, among others. "Very well," she said, stepping forward.

"Just press enter," Arina said, pointing to her keyboard. As she did so, numbers and words began rapidly streaming across the main elevated screen, green text on black.

"Ok," said Arina excitedly. "Kinslaw's account in the Cayman's has been emptied, the money transferred to Steward's business account there.... He's moved it to the phony Kinslaw corporate accounts in Bermuda, the ones we created for him.... Now from each of those to his numbered Swiss account.... And he's apparently withdrawn it all in cash from there." Cheers went up from the cyber warriors. The algorithm had worked to perfection. The whole of it accomplished in less than two minutes.

With a big grin on her face, Arina leaned back in her chair and continued. "The rest will take a few weeks. Cash in amounts small enough not to raise any red flags will be deposited into the various business accounts of Mt. Olympus Enterprises in Geneva. And, in about a month's time, The Bauer Foundation can expect a very large contribution."

"And Kinslaw?" asked Penny.

"Checks they issue will start bouncing once the funds in their American banks are exhausted. Money will still be coming in, so it could take a week or two. Steward will probably be the first to realize what has happened. What he will do, who knows? Report the theft, which he apparently committed? Panic and try to flee the country? Needless to say, Fate will eventually catch up with him."

"It's hard to feel sorry for him," Penny said, "but I do, a little."

"That's because you have a big heart," Michael said. "Just remember what he did to the College of St. Frances and all the people who worked and studied there. Think about the damage by Kinslaw he facilitated. The financial ruin of hundreds of students. The cynical appropriation of public funds to line his own pockets and those of the other Kinslaw executives. As he sowed, so shall he reap. Ours is a just war, if there ever was one."

"Amen," said Frank.

EPILOGUE – MAY 2041

D aphne opened the door of the casita expecting to see her father, but standing there instead was a smiling Hephaestus. "Hello, Daphne," he said. "You look stunning."

She did, of course — she always did, even as a little girl. But now, at 22, she carried herself with a regal bearing, befitting her destiny. The perfectly symmetrical oval face of an Amazon, a narrow and slightly upturned nose, full lips, olive skin, and a dazzling smile. But the similarities to her putative subjects ended there. She had deceptively soft hazel eyes that could darken to the color of storm clouds if provoked, and waves of shoulder-length hair like her mother's, but five natural shades of auburn, as if highlighted by a Hollywood professional.

"Stop it, Harry," she said. "You've just never seen me in a dress. Where's my dad?"

"He went with your mother to the Opera. They have graduation memories to relive. Speaking of which, this is the casita where you were conceived, if I'm not mistaken." He winked.

"Have a look around, if you want. Where are the kids?"

"They're watching a movie in the car — Gal Godot's *Wonder Woman*," he replied, accepting her invitation and stepping inside. "Where's the bedroom?" he asked, raising his eyebrows provocatively.

"Grow up, Harry." She giggled. "How old are you supposed to be these days anyway?"

"Oh, 40ish. But 40 is the new 30, you know. That's certainly true for my lovely wife."

"Your wife and your sister are the two most beautiful women I know."

"They might say the same about you."

"Enough!" she sighed.

"Harry raised his hands in surrender. "Sorry. Marisol loves the compliments; Athena hates them. What's a man to do?"

"Know your audience."

Hephaestus chuckled. "Advice worthy of a queen. Any new thoughts on that front?"

"I don't have to make a decision for a few years yet. Besides, Artemis has the Amazon warriors well in hand, and Themis runs a tight ship on the Island."

"There is the matter of replenishing the troops." A sly smile, with his eyebrows getting still more exercise.

Hers was a rueful smile. "Well, Amazons are no longer dropping like flies, and Helena is getting close to solving the problem of sterility. My only job might be convincing the girls to have sex with men."

"What about you and Ares?"

Daphne laughed. "Not going to happen, ever! And I don't need his immortal genes. Got my own — at least by all appearances. I bet he sent your kids that movie; he gave me a copy when I was their age. Loves to play the villain."

"He did." Harry chuckled.

"Oh, God! I hope we have enough charge left to make it to the Opera. Let me grab my stuff."

"Not to worry," Harry said. "Your grandfather Frank and I designed a system to continuously charge the batteries with solar cells. Can't remember the last time I had to stop at a charging station."

ΩΩΩ

Dr. Penelope Bauer walked toward the podium on the stage of the Santa Fe Opera, having been introduced by Marisol, more properly Dr. Marisol Rivera, Professor of Humanities, and acting President of Zia College. Dr. Rivera had recounted the brief history of the liberal arts school, in just its fourth year of operation, having been built and generously endowed by the Bauer Family Foundation, of which Dr. Bauer was Executive Director. She explained the unique charter governing the College, whereby the Faculty would receive equal salaries and share essential administrative duties on a rotating basis, with much of the daily administrative workload performed by students in lieu of tuition. As an aside, she noted that her term was up, and that she was quite looking forward to relinquishing the responsibilities of President to the next victim. Finally, she spoke briefly of Dr. Bauer's scholarship, notably her Pulitzer Prize-winning book, *The True Olympians*, which had revolutionized the study of classics and cultural evolution. The two women hugged, as befitting their long friendship, and exchanged places, Marisol to sit and Penny to speak.

"Many of you know that my daughter, Daphne, is among the first graduating class of Zia College. She's the one blushing the shade of her mother's hair, sitting just there, in her mortarboard and gown." Penny pointed. "What you may not know is that 23 years ago, I was sitting more or less in the same spot, a member of the last graduating class of the College of St. Frances. Truth be told, I was not in mortar and gown, but in a blue belted sundress that was probably indecently short. The absence of traditional dress that day was because the ceremony had been organized by the students to protest the sale of the College to the Kinslaw Group, a for-profit educational corporation. I am pleased to report that Kinslaw has since gone belly up, and the man most responsible for the sale of the College of St. Frances is sitting behind bars. These facts are traceable in part to the commencement speech given that day.

"My undergraduate mentor, Dr. A. Michael Ambros, a classics professor, gave that speech. He spoke disparagingly of the commodification of higher education, particularly the ascendency of for-profit colleges, and the corresponding decline of liberal arts education — the sale of the College of St. Frances being just one of countless illustrations. Underlying and supporting these trends, he said, was a vision of a good life understood in strictly material terms, against which he juxtaposed an older view rooted in classical Greek thought, a moral or ethical good life devoted to the pursuit of truth and justice.

"I do not wish to romanticize the Hellenic world, for the greatest achievements of that world were literally built on the backs of slaves and reserved in large measure to men of a certain class. But the Greeks did give us the *polis* and the concept of citizenship. Citizens were expected to set aside their material interests, to subordinate their private concerns to the well-being of the community. The *polis* in turn was the arena in which these individuals developed the qualities of character essential to an ethical life — the virtues of temperance, loyalty, courage, and wisdom. The *polis* in short was the schoolhouse of morality — a function in the modern metropolitan world taken on by liberal arts education.

"Those of you familiar with my work will know that shortly after I graduated from the College of St. Frances, I was gifted a set of ancient engravings by a man who was the last of the Olympian gods, or so I argued in *The True Olympians*. Those were the darkest of days, the values of Western civilization collapsing all around, the gods who carried those values fading away. Perhaps he saw in me a sliver of hope. I had, in fact, been deeply moved by that commencement address, already willing to devote my life to a restoration of the liberal arts, given the opportunity. His gift gave me that chance.

"To make a long story short, the engravings made possible the creation of the Bauer Family Foundation, and thanks to generous contributions from many quarters, but especially from my husband's family, Zia College, and many others like it, have been established or supported in this country and throughout the Western world. Now it is your turn, to go forth as citizens, to live an ethical life, and thereby continue the struggle for truth and justice. We have come a long way since the dark days of 2018. Liberal arts institutions are once again thriving, and for-profit colleges have all but disappeared. If we continue on this path to restore the values of the *polis*, but for everyone, perhaps we can revive the Olympian gods, bring them back to life again. And wouldn't that be grand!"

ACKNOWLEDGMENTS

I owe a debt of gratitude to all the folks at Histria Books, and to family and friends, who offered encouragement, support, and critiques of the early drafts. They know who they are.

The inspiration for this work belongs to my students of many years, who are proving the worth of a liberal education, making this world a better place. They too know who they are.

Addison & Highsmith

Other fine works of fiction available from Addison & Highsmith Publishers, a division of Histria Books:

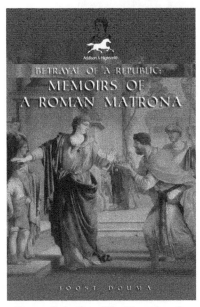

Betrayal of a Republic: Memoirs of a Roman Matrona by Joost Douma

The Lost Diary of Anne Frank by Johnny Teague

Visit

HistriaBooks.com